CRIME C

A Death du Jour M

Hillary Avis

Published by Hilyard Press, Eugene, OR
©2018 Hillary Avis www.hillaryavis.com
ISBN 9781099374760

Cover by Mariah Sinclair www.mariahsinclair.com
For permissions contact: books@hilyardpress.com

Chapter 1

Bethany Bradstreet gazed out the window over her morning coffee. Her shabby rented cottage didn't have many redeeming qualities, but the one thing it did have was a spectacular view of Newbridge. She could see everything from the comfort of her kitchen: the bustling downtown with its quaint brick facades, the charming historic neighborhoods, the smooth blue marina where the fishing boats were already on their way out to sea. A large plume of smoke rose above the town into the pink dawn like a graceful question mark.

She squinted at it. "Hey, isn't that coming from your old neighborhood?"

Her roommate and best friend, Kimmy Caldwell, came over to the window. Unlike Bethany, she'd grown up in Newbridge and knew its back streets like her middle name. "I can't tell. Hang on."

Kimmy rummaged around in the kitchen junk drawer and extracted the small pair of binoculars they kept there to watch the whales spout and breach during their annual migration. She peered through the binoculars in the direction of the smoke as Bethany watched anxiously. "Oh no. Oh no, oh no!"

"What is it?"

Kimmy turned, her face grim. "It's not just my neighborhood—I think it's my house!"

Bethany's stomach knotted. "Are you sure?"

"It has to be—no one else has a giant swan head attached to their front porch! Or what's left of it." Kimmy had grown up

1

in the home belonging to her great-aunt Amara, who was...well, quirky. The swan porch was new and the least of it.

Bethany didn't wait for more information. She twisted her hair into a bun, grabbed her purse, and slipped on her shoes. The world would just have to live with seeing her dancing-banana-print pajama pants. "You want me to drive?"

Kimmy nodded wordlessly and grabbed her jacket on the way out the door. Her blue Honda's engine sputtered when Bethany turned the key, but revved to life with a little gas. They were tense and quiet on the short drive to Amara's house. Out of the corner of her eye, Bethany could see Kimmy lean her head against the window and close her eyes.

Maybe Kimmy was wrong about which house was the source of the smoke. *Please don't let it be hers. Please don't let it be hers.*

Bethany took a deep breath, turned onto Hosanna Street, and immediately slammed on the brakes. The entire street had been cordoned off with police barriers, and a young female officer was waving them to the curb.

Kimmy craned her neck to see around the bank of police cars and fire trucks as Bethany rolled down the driver's side window.

"Where you headed, ma'am?" the officer asked. Her hair was pulled back into a tight ponytail, and she looked like she meant business.

"We saw the smoke—"

"Sorry, no looky-loos. You'll read about the fire in the paper tomorrow." She crossed her arms. "Turn your vehicle around, please."

"But Officer"—Bethany quickly scanned her uniform for a name—"Perez, we're worried it might be—"

Kimmy jumped out of the car, ducked under the barrier, and ran toward the source of the smoke.

"Hey! You can't go in there!" Officer Perez yelled after her. She touched her shoulder walkie. "I got a good citizen headed your way. Southwest sidewalk."

"Roger that," came a voice. "Don't sweat it, Perez."

"Why doesn't anyone ever listen to me?" The cop sighed, clearly annoyed. She looked down at Bethany. "Is it because I'm a woman? Is that why your friend totally ignored me?"

"Uh, no? It's her great-aunt's house. She grew up there, so it's emotional."

"She still should have followed police orders." Officer Perez's face hardened. "Turn your vehicle around. This is a crime scene."

"But I can't just leave her! This is her car, and—wait, what? What do you mean, a crime scene? Is Amara OK?"

"Roll up your window and move your vehicle, *now*."

Just then, a police car pulled up behind Bethany. She motioned to the barrier in front of her car and the cruiser behind her. "I can't!"

Officer Perez rolled her eyes. "Just my luck."

A cop got out of the car and swaggered up to Bethany's window. He put his arm around Officer Perez's shoulders. "This little lady giving you problems, Charley? Want me to handle it?"

Officer Perez shrugged off his embrace. "Nah. Friend of the victim. Just escorting her in." She gave Bethany a meaningful look and jerked her head, motioning for her to get out of the car. "You can man the barrier for a little while, can't you, Coop?"

Coop—or Officer Cooper, judging by his nametag—looked less than enthusiastic about the prospect. Bethany didn't wait for him to protest. She hopped out and started toward the sidewalk, Officer Perez on her heels. When they were out of Coop's earshot, Bethany said, "Thanks for letting me in."

Officer Perez snorted. "Don't think I'm happy about it. I just couldn't stand Coop's smug face for another second. Let *him* play security guard for a while."

Bethany started to grin, but her smile quickly vanished when she caught sight of Kimmy. She was on her knees on the sidewalk in front of her old house—a house that was a smoking, blackened ruin. The giant swan head that once arched proudly above the front door now lay on the lawn, grimy and scorched.

Bethany ran to Kimmy and sank down beside her, ignoring the firefighters and police that swarmed around the street and yard. "Oh, Kimmy. I'm so sorry. I am just *so* sorry."

Kimmy turned toward her, her cheeks streaked with tears. "My poor auntie! What a terrible way to die."

Officer Perez cleared her throat. "If you mean Amara Caldwell, she's just fine. She's over at a neighbor's."

"Oh!" Kimmy rocketed upright and flung her arms around the police officer's neck. Officer Perez froze, a panicked expression on her face, but Kimmy didn't seem to notice. "Thank you! Thank you! I can never thank you enough!"

Bethany's eyes welled up with relief. "Can you take us to her?"

Officer Perez pried Kimmy's arms from around her neck. "Maybe, if you can keep your hands to yourself," she said dryly. "Come on, then."

They followed her two houses down to a picturesque brick colonial with a picket fence in front. Officer Perez knocked at the door and somewhere inside the house, a dog started yapping insistently. The door was swiftly answered by another police officer.

"Family of the victim," Officer Perez said brusquely.

"Oh, Kimberly! Thank the heavens you're here!" The sound of Amara's rich New Orleans patois reached them, and then the woman herself, clad in a flowing green caftan, pushed by the police officer in the doorway and extended her arms. Kimmy rushed into them. Looking over Kimmy's shoulder, Amara spied Bethany on the front walk. "What are you wearing, darling? Are those party clothes?"

Bethany looked down and blushed. "Oh, no. Pajamas."

Officer Perez snickered, and Kimmy withdrew from her great-aunt's arms to glare at the cop. "She rushed out the door to bring me here," she said icily. "You don't need to make fun of her."

Officer Perez held up her hands and took a step off the porch. "No sweat. I'll leave you three to catch up." She turned and, giving Bethany an apologetic grimace, booked it back toward the scene of the fire.

"Fierce. You're even scaring the cops!" Bethany chuckled, and Kimmy grinned sheepishly. The yapping inside the house grew louder, and then a tiny brown ball of fur streaked out the door toward Bethany. Before she could even move, it attacked the hem of her pajama pants, growling and shaking the fabric until it ripped a chunk away.

"Sharky!" Amara commanded from the porch, hands on her hips and her large earrings swinging. The miniature dog bounded back up the steps and leaped into her arms. Bethany stared at her pajama pants, dismayed. The bottom hem of her right leg was completely shredded.

Amara shook her head as she stroked the quivering little animal. "Don't mind that. It's a sign those trousers need to go. You won't keep a man with nightclothes like that, anyway."

"Auntie!" Kimmy protested.

Amara pursed her lips. "I only speak the truth as I see it."

"Don't worry about it. She's right. I think I got these in high school." Bethany gave an internal sigh. *My favorite, most comforting PJs, ruined.* But at least she still had a place to live, unlike poor Amara, whose whole house was destroyed. "Are you OK? What happened?"

"Oh honey, I can't even tell you. I woke up because Sharky was barking in my ear. You're such a good boy, aren't you? Yes, you are! You woke up mama. It was so hot and stuffy, so I went out to the balcony for fresh air. That's when I saw that the house was on fire! Flames everywhere! I couldn't even get down the stairs!"

Kimmy gasped. "What did you do?!"

"Oh, don't worry. The firetrucks came, and they sent two strong gentlemen up the ladder to get me down. I made them go back to get Sharky, and he only bit them a few times, didn't you, sugar? And it didn't even go through their gloves."

"Lucky them," Bethany said wryly. "I'm glad the firetrucks came so quickly when you called!"

"Oh, I didn't call. I didn't even have time. They just appeared. Maybe they had a feeling I would be needing them."

Kimmy rolled her eyes. "Or maybe one of your neighbors called. That seems more likely."

Amara shrugged, extracting her necklace from between Sharky's jaws. "Who am I to say? The universe works in mysterious ways. Won't you come in for some tea, girls?"

Bethany shook her head. "I can't. I have to get to work."

Kimmy's hand flew to her mouth. "Oh, I forgot you're working this morning! Shoot!"

"It's fine. I think I can still make it on time if you drop me off on the way home."

Kimmy bit her lip worriedly. "Will you be OK, Auntie?"

Amara thrust Sharky into Kimmy's hands. "Yes, darling, hold on, I'll get my things." She turned and disappeared down the hall into the house, leaving the door open behind her.

Realization dawned on Bethany. "Is she planning...?"

Kimmy nodded slowly. "I think so."

Bethany groaned. Just what she needed—comments from a judgy relative on a daily basis. She'd moved to Newbridge to get *away* from exactly that! "Do we have any other options?"

"I'm all she's got. Her only other living relative is her sister in Louisiana."

"Friends, maybe?"

"You know her—and you know Sharky." Kimmy giggled, ruffling the dog's fur. "Who's going to invite them to stay?"

"We're not supposed to have pets in the cottage." Bethany furrowed her forehead as she flipped through a mental Rolodex of people who might take Amara in.

Kimmy's face grew serious. "It's just for a few days, until she can get a check from the insurance company for temporary housing. Please say it's OK. She can have my room. I'll sleep on the sofa, and I'll clean up after the dog. She's basically my mom, Bethany."

The look on Kimmy's face was impossible to resist. "Of course—she can stay as long as she needs to. I'll just get some new pajamas."

Chapter 2

Bethany hurriedly looped an apron around her neck and checked the shift assignments. She was on fryer—*again*.

"You're late." Her boss, Alex Vadecki, owner of the Seafood Grotto. She knew it was him without even turning around. *Shoot.* He sounded more than just a little irritated. "Are those pajamas?"

"It was an emergency. My—"

He snapped his fingers. "Nope. Don't want to hear it. This is the third time you've been late in as many weeks."

She turned to face him. "Is that why you put me on the fry station?"

"No, I put you on the fryer because you're good at it."

"What?! You yelled at me when I was on the fryer yesterday!"

Alex leaned in so close she could smell his cologne. "I yelled at you for changing the batter recipe. You fried it just fine." He pointed to her and then to the deep fryer. "Get on your station before I blow a gasket! And don't you dare change the batter again."

Bethany put her hands on her hips. "But I made it better!" she said hotly. "Why don't you want me to make food that actually tastes good?"

"What I *want*"—Alex ran his hand over his slicked-back hair and appeared to be trying to compose himself—"is a consistent customer experience."

"Even if that experience is mediocre?"

9

His face turned the color of a boiled lobster. "Listen, your job is to read the order, dip the fish, fry the fish. Can you do that? If you can't, fine—you can go work elsewhere."

Bethany sighed. "I can do that."

She put on a hairnet and trudged to her station. If he wanted lowest-common-denominator fried food from a classically trained chef, that was his business. *Her* business was learning as much as she could so that she could own her own restaurant someday—and she was learning *a lot* working at the Seafood Grotto. Alex Vadecki was teaching her exactly what *not* to do.

Chapter 3

Monday

After the fight with Alex, nothing went wrong, exactly. But she was forced to send out an endless, soul-killing parade of beige-tasting seafood and french fries. By the end of her shift, she wanted to go home and cry. She clocked out and fished the key to her bike lock from inside her purse as she walked to the bike rack in the parking lot behind the restaurant. When she got there, she was dismayed to see no sign of Daisy, her bright yellow ten-speed. The bike rack was empty.

Stolen?! Adrenaline jolted through her, and she quickly scanned the street in either direction before she remembered that she didn't ride Daisy to work. *Oh, duh, Kimmy dropped me off.*

Now she'd have to ride the bus or walk. *Or maybe...*

She texted Todd Luna, the guy she'd been dating for a couple of months. Things weren't serious yet, but he had a car and worked nearby. Maybe he wouldn't mind running her home. His reply came immediately.

Todd: At Café Sabine for dinner. Join me?

Bethany: OK. I'll walk over. See you in 10.

She sniffed her armpits—not too bad considering she'd just finished scrubbing out a deep fryer. As she walked briskly toward the café, she swiped on some lip balm and then shook her hair out of its bun and fluffed the ends. She caught a glimpse of herself in a storefront window and wasn't too dismayed. Wavy auburn hair framed her face, the black V-neck hugged her curves...annnnd she still had banana-print pajama pants on.

Cringeworthy. Thank goodness she wore a T-shirt to bed last night instead of the matching PJ top—hopefully the long white tablecloths at Café Sabine would hide her pants before Todd noticed. He was a guy, after all.

She rounded the last corner and pushed open the etched-glass door of the restaurant. Using the front entrance felt strange. Normally when she came to Café Sabine, she went through the back door in the alley—the door that went straight to the kitchen—because she was visiting Kimmy, who worked as the café's sous chef. But Kimmy had the day off today, and this time Bethany was a customer, not just a visitor. She had a *date*.

The maître d' sniffed primly and looked her up and down. "Table for one? There may be a wait."

Bethany rolled her eyes. "Don't pretend you don't know me, Thierry. I'm here to meet Todd."

Thierry pursed his lips, but picked up a menu from the stand. "Follow me. The gentleman is already seated."

It seemed like Thierry purposely led her on a meandering course through the entire café. Bethany held her bag below her waist, hoping that it might block other diners' view of her unusual attire, and tried not to bump too many diners' chairs with it along the way. Everyone seated at the dimly lit restaurant was well-dressed, as the café catered to the lawyers and financiers who worked downtown—people like Todd. Despite her strategic handbag maneuvers, a few people noticed her pants and tittered as she passed.

She glared at them, but pasted on a smile as she approached Todd's table. He rose when he saw her, and she was horrified to see another man stand up beside him. He wasn't eating alone.

So much for a romantic dinner! She clenched her teeth, still smiling, and sat down quickly without shaking the strange man's extended hand, praying that neither of them noticed all the dancing bananas printed on her lower half.

Todd leaned to give her a quick embrace, and she suppressed a gag. He was wearing some kind of new cologne that must have been designed to evoke a new car—it basically smelled like gasoline.

"Why are you being so rude?" he asked in a low voice so the other man wouldn't hear. He pulled back to look at her and she shrugged, still fake smiling. He pasted on a smile, too, and turned back to his companion. "Bethany's a top notch chef, trained at the Culinary Institute in New Haven. You should taste her clam chowder, Don—it puts this place to shame."

"Actually, they use my recipe here," Bethany said smoothly, concealing her irritation with Todd. He had no business criticizing the food at Café Sabine—Kimmy was one of the best chefs in Newbridge.

Don burst into laughter, his belly jiggling. "Don Hefferman. I like your spunk. You two are quite the power couple."

Bethany was taken aback. *Power couple?* A fry cook and a junior real estate developer? What had Todd told Don about her?

"Don's my investment partner," Todd said.

Thierry, still standing expectantly beside the table, cleared his throat. "Shall I bring the champagne, sir?"

Todd nodded and winked at Bethany. Her stomach clenched and her heart thudded in her chest. *He's not going to propose, is he?!* She liked the guy—he was handsome, successful, and charming—but it was way too soon! "Um, why the celebration?" She tried to make her voice light, but it came out shrill and quavering.

"This is a big moment in our lives. I have a little surprise for you." Todd leaned down to get something out of his satchel. *A ring?!*

She scraped back her chair and glanced over her shoulder at the exit. She had half a mind to just run out of the restaurant. "Um...I'm not sure I'm ready for this. I mean, we haven't known each other that long."

Don shifted in his seat and chuckled uncomfortably. "Maybe I ought to excuse myself, give you two some privacy?"

Todd sat up just as Thierry returned with a bottle of bubbly and three glasses. "No, I want you both to be here."

Bethany shot a panicked look at Don while Thierry filled their glasses. He shrugged at her, a bead of sweat dripping down his forehead. Poor guy—he was as anxious to avoid a proposal scene as she was. "Why don't we do this another time?"

Todd's smile was still as broad and bright as ever, but his eyes narrowed. Was he having second thoughts about popping the question? Bethany hoped so. He picked up his champagne flute. "The bubbles won't hold, hon. It's now or never."

She sighed and picked up her glass, her stomach already queasy at the thought of rejecting him so publicly. "Ready or not, here you come."

Don snorted. Todd turned and raised his eyebrows questioningly, and Don quickly coughed to cover the noise and lifted his own glass.

"A toast to new beginnings," Todd said loudly. "For all of us!"

Bethany and Don exchanged a puzzled look. Todd pulled a stack of paper from his lap. The top sheet was filled with official-looking stamps and signatures. *It wasn't a ring.* Bethany breathed a sigh of relief and took a sip of her champagne, but then stopped mid-sip. The papers looked an awful lot like a contract. Not...*a marriage contract?* Was Todd suggesting they do the deed right here and now, with Don as a witness? *New beginnings, a big day for us...what else could it be?*

Bethany stood up and backed away from the table in horror.

Todd squinted at her. "Are those...*bananas?*"

Mortified, she plopped back down in her chair, covered her lap with the tablecloth, and slugged down the rest of the champagne. She took a deep breath and let it out slowly. "I'm ready. Hit me."

Don and Todd stared at her, both frozen with their glasses in their hands. Finally Todd cocked his head to the side and asked in a puzzled voice, "Are you OK?"

She nodded. "Fine. Just say what you're going to say—I won't stop you." She closed her eyes and gritted her teeth.

Todd clinked his glass against Don's. "The city greenlighted our condo development! We're good to go! We'll break ground on Wednesday."

Don's eyes widened. "What? I thought that the historical society had killed the project."

"I know! Lucky for us, the city council pushed it through this afternoon."

Bethany slumped in her chair. *Phew. Not a proposal.* Don just looked uncomfortable.

Todd glanced from her to Don and back again. "Come on you two! Let's celebrate!"

Don rubbed his bald head. "Sorry, it's just a big surprise. Cheers, Todd." He tossed back his whole glass of champagne just like Bethany had and pulled the papers over in front of him.

Why wasn't he as happy about this as Todd seemed to be? Bethany studied Don as he studied the signatures.

The smile on Todd's face had completely faded from his eyes, even though his mouth was still stretched into a grimace. He turned to her. "How about you?"

"Congrats. I'm happy for you, really."

He tossed up his hands. "Maybe I didn't explain this meeting very well. We're going to convert the old church into live-work condos, but there will be retail space on the bottom floor. Don's been looking to invest in a restaurant concept—right, Don?—and what better place to invest than the condo development! I wanted you two to meet so Don could hear about your restaurant concept, Bethy!"

She cringed a little at the nickname. That's what her parents called her when they were being condescending. *Don't you want to think that through, Bethy? What's your backup plan, Bethy?* But unlike her parents, Todd wanted her to achieve her dreams. Too bad she didn't actually *have* a restaurant concept. She hadn't planned on taking that step until she was an experienced sous chef—at least five years down the road!

She stumbled over her words. "Wow, I wish I'd known—I'd have prepared a little more. I'm sorry I don't have any materials for you, Don."

"Don't worry about it," Don said, shaking his head. "I wasn't expecting this, either!"

"He thought he was getting out of this deal!" Todd punched him lightly on the shoulder. "Didn't you, Donny? But now he's stuck with me."

Bethany raised her eyebrows. "What do you mean?"

"Ah, nothing." Don chuckled uncomfortably. "Happy that the deal went through. It's going to be great for Newbridge—we'll get some of those start-up kids into our condos and bring that neighborhood into the twenty-first century."

Todd grinned at Bethany. "Told you—it's the perfect location for a cutting-edge eatery with Newbridge's hottest young chef at the helm!"

Bethany wondered what he meant by "cutting edge." That new molecular gastronomy, where the food was all shaped like origami and made of beet powder? That was definitely *not* a concept she'd pitch to Don. Her style leaned more toward comfort food, and she was pretty sure Todd didn't mean mac-n-cheese. Still, she didn't want to let the opportunity slip through her fingers.

"I can put together a proposal for you, if you're interested."

Don nodded. "Sounds good."

Todd leaned forward across the table. "I can do you one better. You can taste her food for yourself on Wednesday. Bethany's going to cater the groundbreaking party!"

"I am?" Bethany blinked. Todd glared at her. "I mean, I am! I'll have a tasting menu for you to try on...?"

"Wednesday evening," Todd finished.

"Wednesday," she echoed. *Forty-eight hours away—can I pull it off?* Her mind started racing, mentally calculating all the tasks involved. She needed tables, linens, cutlery and china, warmers—and somewhere to cook, not to mention a menu. She had to find time to go shop and somewhere to store her ingredients. And she had to work her daily shifts at the Seafood Grotto! She groaned internally.

Don's voice brought her back to the moment. "I'll see you two on Wednesday, then! Is this my copy?" He tapped the papers in front of him.

Todd nodded. "I'll get the bill. Glad to be doing business with you, Don. We're going to make a bucket of cash."

The two men shook hands as Don gathered the paperwork and said goodbye to Bethany. She waited until Don was all the way out of the restaurant before she turned to Todd.

"It would have been nice to have a heads up on this whole thing before I showed up in my pajamas!"

Todd's smile disappeared. "I could say the same! I drop this opportunity in your lap and your lap is full of dancing bananas! And then you were so rude to my investor—who could be *your* investor if you play your cards right. What were you thinking?"

Bethany crossed her arms. "I was *thinking* that my best friend's childhood home burned down last night, so I didn't have time to get dressed before we rushed out the door this morning. I was *thinking* that my boyfriend invited me to a romantic dinner, and that maybe he wouldn't care about my PJs so much because he'd be too busy looking into my eyes. I was *thinking* you were going to propose and I was trying to give you an out." She bit her lip, afraid she'd said too much, but Todd just laughed.

"You thought the champagne was for a proposal?"

She nodded, her cheeks flushing. "I thought it was too early, and I didn't want to hurt your feelings by saying no."

He laughed again, louder. "Trust me, even if I wanted to, I wouldn't propose to you when you go out in public smelling like a french fry and wearing *that*!"

Her cheeks grew even hotter and her eyes stung with tears. Todd's face fell. "I'm sorry—I didn't mean it like that. I just meant that if I proposed to someone, I'd make sure it was the right moment. You know me—perfectionist to the core."

Message received—I'm not perfect. Bethany sighed and scrubbed the tears from her cheeks with her white linen napkin.

He reached across the table and chucked her chin. "Don't cry, Bethy."

"I'm not crying," she said automatically. "I'm just tired. It's been a long day, and I have no idea how to pull off this catering gig you dumped on me."

"Dumped on you? You should be happy. Don's a big-name investor, and he's going to taste *your* food! This is your big break!" Todd's voice was loud and brittle. "Tons of heavy hitters are going to be there on Wednesday. If you don't come through, I'm going to look like a fool. And nobody will take you seriously, either. You'll be a fry cook forever."

Maybe not forever—Alex Vadecki would be happy to fire me any time, and my parents would love to see me in another profession. But she'd be miserable giving up on her dream of being a restaurateur someday. Todd was the only person besides Kimmy who really understood and supported her ambitions. She sighed. "I know. I won't let you down. I'll figure out a way to pull it off—somehow."

Chapter 4

Monday

Todd stopped the car in front of her tiny cottage and leaned over to kiss her cheek. "You can thank me when you get your first Michelin star."

"Will do." There were light years between catering a real estate developer's party and earning a Michelin star, but Todd wasn't in the industry. He didn't know that ambition couldn't substitute for experience. "Maybe then you won't have to lie to people about my job anymore." She winced—that had come out harsher than she intended.

"Aw, be sweet, Bethy."

She rolled her eyes at the nickname, feeling more salty than sweet, and stepped out into the night. He flashed her a charming smile through the open door, and she relented somewhat. "Thanks for the ride—and everything."

"I just want what's best for my girl."

Bethany nodded. "I know." The quiet dark was split by a wail coming from inside the cottage, and it sent her pulse racing. She turned and dashed inside.

The living room was dim except for a circle of candles that flickered on the coffee table, their glow illuminating two figures huddled on the sofa. Amara sat with her face in her hands, and Kimmy had her arm protectively over her great-aunt's shoulders. Sharky lay curled in Amara's lap, quivering with nervous energy.

Bethany dropped her purse and kneeled in front of them, her jaw tight with concern. "What's going on? Is everything

OK?" Sharky growled at her and she scooted back a little bit in case he was thinking about launching at her. She'd already seen what the little dog could do to a pair of pajama pants, and she didn't want to know what he could do to her throat.

Amara raised her head, her cheeks streaked with tears. "My home, my home! What will I do?" She wailed again and rocked back and forth where she sat, clutching Sharky to her chest.

Kimmy's face crumpled at the sight of her aunt's despair, and Bethany reached out to squeeze her free hand. "I'm so sorry. Has she been like this all day?"

"Let me get you some water, Auntie." Kimmy stood up and nodded toward the kitchen, and Bethany followed her. When they were far enough away that Amara was out of earshot, Kimmy spoke in a low voice. "She wasn't like this until just now. The police came to tell her that the fire investigator ruled it an arson!"

Bethany gasped. "Someone lit her house on fire—while she was in it?"

Kimmy nodded as she retrieved a glass from the cupboard and filled it with ice cubes. "She could have been killed. And worse, the cops don't believe her. They think she did it!"

"What? Why would she set her own house on fire?"

"Insurance fraud, I guess. Which means she can't get any insurance money until they investigate and clear her." Kimmy filled the glass at the sink.

Bethany looked over to where Amara sat cuddling Sharky as he gnawed on the arm of the sofa. "Let me guess—that means she has to stay here."

"Just until we can find her somewhere else." Kimmy's eyes were pleading. "She's my only family—I can't put her in a hotel."

"No, of course not. She should stay here." Bethany felt slightly ashamed of herself for her reluctance to host Amara, especially when she'd done so much for Kimmy. But with one look at the sofa, Bethany nearly changed her mind. Sharky was ferociously attacking one of the throw pillows and had already wormed shreds of stuffing out of the center. "What about the dog, though? We're not supposed to have pets."

Kimmy looked thoughtful. "If the property management company notices, we can say he's just visiting. And we'll make sure he's never in the house alone. Amara takes Sharky with her everywhere, anyway."

"How long do you think it'll be?"

Kimmy shrugged. "Depends on how long it takes the police to investigate the arson, I guess." She walked back to the sofa and handed Amara the glass. "Here you go, Auntie."

Bethany joined them in the cottage's cozy living room, perching in her favorite chenille easy chair and curling her feet under her. Amara choked on her ice water, spraying droplets everywhere. She motioned urgently until Kimmy retrieved a paper towel so her aunt could dab the front of her caftan. Then she shook the soggy wad at Bethany.

"You'll get a crooked back sitting like that! Pain will follow you for the rest of your life." Amara delivered the words in her resonant fortuneteller's voice, making it sound like a prophecy rather than posture advice.

"She'll be OK for one night," Kimmy said, nabbing the paper towel from Amara's hand and tossing it in the waste basket.

"That's what you think, but you're still just children."

The buzz of irritation skittered across Bethany's scalp as she put her feet flat on the floor and struggled to keep her tongue in check. *How many days can I put up with this person?*

Amara coughed violently and then waved her hand in front of her face like she was wafting away smoke. "That fire is still in my lungs. I can feel it burning me from the inside."

Bethany sighed. *Poor Amara.* No wonder she was so snappish—her whole life had been destroyed. It was just lucky that she and Sharky had made it out in time. The idea of enduring a long investigation before she could start to rebuild her home must be excruciating. *For her and for us.*

Now that Bethany thought about it, a short investigation would mean Amara—and her destructive little dog—would be out of the cottage sooner rather than later. *Win-win.*

Bethany leaned forward in her chair. "Who do you think might have done this? Is anyone angry with you?"

"I don't worry about other people's opinions too much." Amara sniffed. "It's none of my business what they think of me. I just carry on."

Kimmy rolled her eyes. "Maybe you should worry a little bit, Auntie. Someone destroyed your house! There has to be a reason."

Amara stroked Sharky's head while she extracted some pillow stuffing from between his teeth. "Well. It's true that George is not too pleased with me. He left a letter in my mailbox last week that said he would kill Sharky if I didn't keep him out of his garden."

Kimmy gasped. "He didn't!"

"Who's George?" Bethany asked.

"George Washington, her next-door neighbor. He's a grumpy old guy, but I didn't think he'd hurt Sharky."

Amara shrugged. "He said he would. Maybe he set that fire to kill us both. Now his prize dahlias won't be disturbed."

"I'm not sure." Kimmy leaned over and tousled Sharky's fur. "I've known Mr. Washington for my whole life, and that seems pretty extreme, even for him."

"You never really know someone," Amara said darkly.

"Do you still have the note?" Bethany asked.

Amara nodded. "Here in my purse." She dug out a folded piece of paper and held it out. Bethany opened it and read the words that were scrawled jaggedly in permanent marker.

YOU DON'T KNOW SQUAT ABOUT BEING A GOOD NEIGHBOR. KEEP THAT DOG LEASHED OR YOU MIGHT NOT SEE IT AGAIN. G.

Bethany flipped the sheet over and saw that the note was written on the back of a flyer advertising a meeting of the New-bridge Historical Society. "You should give this to the police! It could be evidence." She handed the note to Kimmy so that she could read it, too.

Kimmy skimmed it quickly and sighed with relief. "It doesn't say he was going to kill Sharky, Auntie. I knew he wouldn't do something like that."

Amara pursed her lips and held Sharky up in front of her like a baby. "It said I wouldn't see you again, didn't it, love? What else could it mean?"

Bethany furrowed her forehead, thinking. "It does seem sinister. What does he mean, 'you don't know squat about be-ing a good neighbor'? Is that just about the dog?"

Amara put Sharky down on the floor and shrugged, her earrings swinging. "Who knows. Old men complain about everything. He didn't like my beautiful swan porch, he didn't like my dog, and he didn't like that I am friendly to everyone."

Sharky started gnawing on the leg of the coffee table, making a horrible grating sound against the wood. Bethany nudged him with her toe to get him to stop, but he just growled at her with the table leg still in his mouth, and she didn't press her luck.

Kimmy laughed disbelievingly. "What? How would friendliness make you a bad neighbor? That makes no sense. I'm starting to think Mr. Washington is getting senile."

Amara sat back on the sofa, seemingly unaware that Sharky was attempting to fell the coffee table with his teeth. "You know how it is. You like someone they don't like, and they call you an enemy."

"Ah, there's the real story." Kimmy gave Amara the side-eye. "Go on, tell us—who has his goat?"

"Who doesn't?" Amara shrugged again. "He even had that terrible woman from the historical society bothering me."

"What woman?" Bethany asked, surreptitiously taking notes on her phone.

"She means Fancy Peters, the president of the historical society," Kimmy explained. "She's been harassing Auntie since she built her swan porch. You've probably seen her around town. She's the one who rides the old-fashioned tricycle and wears antique clothes."

Bethany wrote down the name. "I think I've seen her at the restaurant. Why doesn't she like the porch, though? Isn't that swan head antique?"

Amara nodded. "It was part of the largest carousel in New Orleans—we called them flying horses even though they were all kinds of animals. My swan was carved in Paris, France, in 1918 and then shipped all the way across the sea as a gift to celebrate the city's two-hundredth birthday. It was painted—"

"With real gold," Kimmy finished. "Don't get her started on the swan. The historical society was ticked off about the porch addition because our house—Auntie's house—was a safehouse for escaped slaves before the Civil War. All renovations and additions are supposed to be approved by the society to make sure they are historically accurate."

Amara waved her hand. "Screened porches are a necessity! Even in 1850, mosquitos were biting people. I don't know what bug flew up her—"

"Auntie!"

"I was going to say skirt." Amara finally noticed the little dog's destruction and pried Sharky's jaws from the coffee table. The leg had been reduced to what looked like a bundle of toothpicks. "She came by yesterday evening to say that I shouldn't be allowed to inhabit such an important piece of Newbridge history. She said I didn't deserve my own home! I was so angry, I—"

Kimmy gasped. "You didn't hit her, did you?"

Amara pursed her lips and frowned. "I don't engage in such nonsense, child. I told her to stop living in the past. And I said she looks like someone's mail-order bride in those puffed sleeves and petticoats."

"You didn't!" Kimmy looked horrified. "No wonder George said you're a bad neighbor!"

Amara sat up straight and looked straight ahead, avoiding Kimmy's gaze. "That woman doesn't live on my street. She's no neighbor of mine."

Bethany broke in. "Do you think this Fancy person was mad enough about the porch to set your house on fire?"

Kimmy shook her head firmly. "No way! The historical society is interested in preserving history, not destroying it."

Amara put her hand on Kimmy's arm to stop her from saying more, and leaned toward Bethany. "Who can say? Maybe she was trying to scare me out of town."

Kimmy looked skeptical, but Bethany saved the two names in her phone to give to the police. One of them might very well be the arsonist.

Chapter 5

Tuesday

HISTORIC HOME BURNS
By Robin Ricketts

Newbridge, CT—In what Fire Marshall Miller has deemed "the clearest case of arson" he'd ever seen, a 200-year-old Hosanna Street home went up in smoke Sunday night. Owner Amara Caldwell sobbed outside the smoking wreck of her former residence on Monday morning while clutching her beloved pet.

"I barely escaped with my life," Caldwell claimed.

Police continue to investigate but have not released the names of any suspects. No clear motive for the arson has emerged.

• • • •

"THAT'S ALL THEY PRINTED about it." Bethany put the newspaper beside her breakfast plate.

"*Claimed*?" Amara spat out. "*Claimed*? How can they call my house a smoking wreck and then imply that my life wasn't in danger?" She pulled the crust off her toast and tossed it under the table where Sharky gobbled it up.

"If they can't confirm your story with another source, they can't print it as fact," Bethany explained. "They just say 'claimed' because they have to take your word for it."

"Don't worry about it too much." Kimmy brought three cups of coffee over to the table. "It's not like the *Newbridge*

Community Observer is exactly the *Times*. Probably some college kid wrote the article."

A loud knock at the door made her jump just as she was setting down the mugs, and the coffee sloshed all over the table. She dove for a kitchen towel, and Bethany rose to answer the door.

"Who the heck is here at seven thirty in the morning?" She ran her hand through her hair, hoping it didn't look like an unpruned hedge. At least her pajamas were slightly more passable as regular clothes than yesterday's—these had a giant giraffe head printed on one leg instead of dancing bananas.

She opened the door and saw two cops standing awkwardly on the front porch. The cottage's porch was so small that the two officers had to crowd together until they looked joined at the hip. Bethany recognized both of them. One was Officer Perez, the woman who had tried to stop them from entering Hosanna Street yesterday. The other looked familiar, but she couldn't remember his name.

"Officer Cooper," he said, extending his hand. Ah, yes, the smug one who had razzed Officer Perez. Bethany wondered how she felt about being paired with him. From the looks of her, not too happy. "This is my junior partner, Charlene Perez."

"Call me Charley."

Bethany shook Officer Cooper's hand and smiled at Charley, who smiled back.

"We need to speak with Amara Caldwell. Is she here?" Cooper asked.

Bethany nodded. "Come on in. We're having breakfast. You want some coffee?"

"Please," Charley said gratefully. "We didn't have time to stop before we came over. Cream and sugar."

"Just black for me. None of that girly stuff." Officer Cooper chuckled, elbowing his partner.

Bethany rolled her eyes and poured two cups of steaming coffee from the pot, swirling cream and sugar into one of them. As the cops pulled up chairs to the kitchen dinette, she handed each of them their cups. With a fierce growl, Sharky leaped down from Amara's lap and attacked Officer Cooper's boot-laces. The portly cop yelped in surprise and almost tipped his chair over backward as he scooted away from the ferocious little dog.

"Oh no!" Kimmy scrambled under the table and grabbed Sharky, holding him at arm's length while he yammered and drooled, trying to get to Officer Cooper. "Let me shut him in the bathroom so he doesn't bother us."

Amara sipped her coffee, her eyes fixed on the table's red laminate top. She hadn't greeted the officers or even acknowledged they were there! Worried that they were making a poor impression, Bethany cleared her throat and asked, "What can we do for you?"

Cooper smiled, trying to catch Amara's eye, but she studiously avoided making eye contact. "Well, we just came to tell Amara here that we've released the scene. You can go back to collect any personal items."

Kimmy returned from the bathroom in time to overhear his remarks and put her hand on Amara's arm. "I can drive you over there, Auntie."

"Is anything left?" Bethany asked.

Charley nodded. "Some of the rooms toward the back of the house are just smoke-damaged. The staircase and second floor aren't safe, though."

"You ladies be careful, now," Cooper admonished. "Don't take risks just to retrieve your favorite lipstick."

Amara looked up, her eyes glittering. "I don't need your advice about visiting my own home. You've delivered your message, and now you can go."

Kimmy clutched her great-aunt's arm more tightly and smiled at the cops. "So sorry. It has been a difficult couple of days."

Officer Cooper raised his eyebrows and sat back in his chair. "Oh, we're not going anywhere just yet. We have a few questions for you about the fire. You said you were sleeping?"

Amara nodded. "Sound asleep."

"So you didn't hear anything or see anything unusual before you went to bed?"

Bethany waited for Amara to tell the officer about the threatening note and the visit from the historical society lady, but she just shook her head firmly.

"No, no, all as usual."

Why didn't Amara mention the potential suspects? *Maybe she has altercations with her neighbors on a daily basis.* She might not think it was out of the ordinary, but Bethany certainly did! And the cops needed to know what was going on in the neighborhood if they were going to figure out who set the fire.

"It wasn't exactly a normal afternoon. Sorry, Amara, but it wasn't. She received a threat from her neighbor George Washington."

"It wasn't a threat!" Kimmy said. "It was just a note. A reminder to keep her dog out of his yard."

"Do you have the note?" Officer Cooper asked, fishing an evidence bag out of his utility belt.

Amara sighed and put her huge tapestry purse on the table, riffling through it to find the note. "It's in here somewhere—you'll just have to wait for me to go through it all."

"We got time," Charley said, leaning forward and putting her elbows on the table. Officer Cooper shot her a look that said *not that much time*.

"While you're waiting, there's someone else you should take a look at." Bethany pulled out her phone to check the name she'd written down. "Fancy Peters. She's president of the historical society, right, Kimmy? And she stopped by Amara's house on Sunday evening to complain about the new addition."

Charley smirked. "The giant swan head?"

"The whole screened porch," Kimmy explained.

"It was a gift from France!" Amara said loudly, finally producing what looked like a shredded napkin from her purse. Officer Cooper held out the evidence bag and she dropped it inside.

He smoothed the note inside the clear bag and looked up at her. "What is this, a joke?"

Bethany peered over his shoulder. It was the same note Amara had shown her the night before, but it was nearly unrecognizable. The writing was smeared and half of the paper was missing altogether! "What happened?!"

Kimmy and Amara exchanged a look, as if each were daring the other to speak. Amara was pure steel, her eyes narrowed to slits, so of course Kimmy broke first. "Sharky," she said, looking as guilty as if she had chewed up the paper herself. The little dog must have heard his name, because Bethany heard him yapping even though he was down the hall and behind the bathroom door.

Cooper stared at her in disbelief. "You're telling me that the dog ate the evidence?"

Kimmy nodded, looking miserable, while Amara trained her gaze on the light fixture and complete avoided eye contact with anyone at the table.

The cop threw the evidence bag down on the table. "This is trash! We can't even read it!"

Charley slid the bag toward herself. "I'm sure we can get something from it. Doesn't hurt to try, anyway. We appreciate you turning this over to us, don't we, Coop?"

Cooper's face had lost all of its smug humor. He only had eyes for Amara, and his voice was cold. "We'll find whoever set this fire. Doesn't matter how long it takes or how much we get jerked around, we'll find 'em."

Bethany swiped through the notes on her phone. "Hey, I wrote down what the note said. Here it is."

Cooper sneered. "That's what you say it said. A little convenient that you didn't take a photo, isn't it? Why should we believe you?"

Charley rose from the table and cleared her throat. "Email what the note said to me. Think of anything else and let us know, OK?" She handed a business card to Kimmy and pointed to the email address on it, and then to the telephone number listed. "And that's my direct line. You can call me for updates on the investigation."

"They can call the non-emergency line at the station," Cooper said, pushing his chair back from the table.

"OK," Kimmy said, slipping the card into her purse that was sitting on the counter. "We won't pester you."

"It's fine," Charley assured her. "You are the victims here, and we want to make sure you're taken care of."

Cooper snorted, and muttered under his breath, "Dog ate the evidence, my hat."

Amara's steady gaze at the light fixture wavered for a moment, and a vein pulsed in her forehead—she looked about to blow. Bethany jumped up from her seat. "Why don't I show you out?"

She walked the officers to the cottage door and held it open for them. Cooper went straight to the squad car parked out front, but Charley paused for a moment in the doorway.

"I have to say, I was surprised to see you here. I knew the vic—I mean, I knew Amara Caldwell was staying with her niece, but I didn't realize you lived here, too. Are you and Ms. Caldwell...an item?"

Bethany shook her head. "We're just roommates. We met in culinary school and have lived together ever since."

"Perez! Get a move on!" Cooper shouted from the car.

Charley stepped out onto the porch. "Any boyfriends, exes hanging around?"

"No—I mean, Kimmy broke up with her girlfriend a few months ago, but it was friendly."

"What about you?"

Bethany blushed, thinking of the humiliating date she'd had the night before. "I'm seeing someone. He's in real estate here in town."

"Is it serious?"

Not serious enough for a proposal. "Not really."

"But he knows Ms. Caldwell. Does he know her family?"

Bethany shrugged. "He eats at her restaurant and knows her name, but I don't think they've ever had a real conversation. I doubt he even knows she grew up in Newbridge."

"Perez!" Officer Cooper had his arm out the window of the squad car and was drumming his fingers on the side of the door.

Charley glanced over her shoulder at him. "I should go. One thing—if you think of anyone else who has a grudge against Ms. Caldwell *or* her aunt, can you call me? Sometimes it's hard for victims to be objective about people they like. It could be helpful to have your perspective on their inner circle." She handed Bethany another copy of her business card.

Bethany nodded. "I'll do that." She watched Charley walk down the path to the police car and slide into the passenger seat. It was hard to know whether the two cops had some kind of schtick going, or if they really had such different communication styles. Cooper seemed like he'd made up his mind that Amara was involved in the arson, while Charley had been more understanding. But the conversation on the porch seemed different, like maybe Charley thought that Amara was withholding information—or that Bethany was.

As the police car drove away and she stared at the business card in her hand, she realized something. *If they're looking at Amara's inner circle for potential suspects, they're looking at me.*

Chapter 6

From where Bethany stood on the sidewalk, Amara looked like a ghost haunting a graveyard. Her back bent, she moved slowly through the wreckage of her former home with Sharky tucked underneath one arm, using her cane to poke through the piles of belongings the fire department had salvaged from the ashes. Half-burned books, smoky glassware, cracked statues, and withered houseplants dotted the blackened front lawn.

Kimmy stowed a cardboard box of cookware in the trunk of her car. "Do you think we can get the swan on the roof rack?"

Bethany shook her head. "I tried lifting it and the thing weighs a ton! I mean, literally. I couldn't even budge it. We'll have to get some kind of forklift to move it, and even then I don't know where we'd move it *to*."

"I'm sure she will want to put it back on the house when she rebuilds. We'll just need to store it until then."

"Does she even want to rebuild? Maybe she should use the insurance money to move somewhere else." Bethany eyed the neighboring houses. In more than one window, she spied on-lookers—none of whom had come out to express sympathy to Amara for the loss of her home nor to offer help with the salvage efforts. "It doesn't seem like she has many friends on Hosanna Street."

"She's lived here for twenty years—I doubt she'd want to be anywhere else." Kimmy loaded a box of knick-knacks into the car and used her shoulder to wipe the soot off her forehead. "These people know her, and they know me. They don't wish our family any harm. They're probably just nervous. Who knows what that Officer Cooper has been saying when he questions people, or how the arson investigators were treating them yesterday. In this neighborhood, nobody wants to get mixed up in police business. They'll come out of their houses once this investigation is over."

Bethany nodded. "At least the other cop, Charley, seems nice. She acts fair, like she hasn't made up her mind already."

"Exactly. She *acts* fair. Who knows what she really thinks, though. What if they blame this on Auntie just so they can close the case?"

"Hey. Hey." Bethany put her arm around Kimmy's shoulders and squeezed. "This is all going to work out. They'll figure out who set the fire, Amara will get her insurance payout, and then she'll be able to rebuild her life. Sharky will probably get a deluxe doghouse out of the deal."

The joke coaxed a grin out of Kimmy. "I hope you're right. Oh!" Her smile vanished as she noticed something over Bethany's shoulder. Bethany turned to see what had caught her eye. An older man was shuffling up the side yard between his house and Amara's.

"Is that the guy who sent the note? George?"

Kimmy nodded. "I've always called him Mr. Washington. I hope we didn't get him into too much trouble with the cops."

Bethany watched him unlock a small shed and retrieve a garden hoe. He carefully relocked the shed and began scraping the weeds from around the edges of a flower bed, never once greeting Amara or even glancing in her direction.

"For someone concerned about neighborliness, he doesn't seem too worried about what happened to his neighbor."

Kimmy sighed and leaned her head on Bethany's shoulder. "He was really kind to me after my parents died. He used to let me come over and watch cartoons after school because Auntie would never let us get a TV. I feel so terrible that he's been caught up in this!"

"I wonder what excuse he'll make for that mean note when the police question him."

Kimmy's hand flew to her mouth. "Oh! I should warn him that they'll be coming." She started toward the yard.

"Kimberly!" Amara stood on the lawn holding Sharky held away from her body with two hands. "He needs to potty! Will you take him? I have to finish sorting the silver."

Kimmy sighed and made a face at Bethany. "We really don't have time for this."

Bethany glanced at the clock on her phone. Kimmy was right. They needed to leave in the next fifteen minutes or she'd be late to work—again. "I can go talk to him if you want. That way we'll all be ready to go in a few minutes."

"Would you? Just tell him I sent you." Kimmy raised her voice so Amara could hear her fifteen yards away and called, "Coming, Auntie!"

Bethany nodded and cut across the grass to where the man was chopping some delicate pink flowers underneath a lilac bush. She cleared her throat as she approached so she wouldn't surprise him. "Um, hi. Mr. Washington?"

He glanced over his shoulder at her and then resumed hacking the pretty plants, scraping the ground around the blooming shrub down to bare earth. As he broke the roots and crushed the stems, the plants emitted a sharp, familiar smell that Bethany couldn't place.

"Little Kimmy sent you." The way he said it wasn't a question. He must have been watching them even though he acted like he wasn't paying attention.

"Yes, she wanted to let you know—"

"That ol' Amara thinks I torched her porch?" He straightened up and winked at her.

"No! I mean, I don't know what she thinks. But Kimmy wanted me to tell you that the police might be by to ask about that note you left in the mailbox."

He froze, his forehead furrowed. "Oh. That. Amara gave it to the cops?"

"Yeah. But Sharky got ahold of it, so there's not much left. Can't even read what you wrote."

He chuckled. "What a shame."

Bethany swallowed. Before she could stop herself, she blurted out, "I know what you wrote, though. I saw it before the dog ate it. And I copied it down word-for-word."

He turned to face her, the humor evaporating from his expression. "And?"

She eyed his hoe and took a step backward so she was out of range if he decided to swing it at her. "You sounded angry. Were you?"

He thumped the hoe on the dirt. "Darn right I was! You would be too if that critter was chewing up everything you own!"

Bethany thought of the eviscerated throw pillow currently on her sofa, right next to the coffee table with only three functional legs. It wasn't a stretch to imagine why someone would bear ill will toward Sharky. "So you threatened to kill the dog so she'd keep him inside?"

"Nah, I wouldn't hurt the little stinker. I just meant she might not see him again if he ran off. She ought to keep him on a leash. Out of my yard *and* safe."

Bethany nodded. *Maybe Kimmy was right—maybe the note wasn't a threat at all.* "You could just build a fence."

George snorted. "Tell that to the historical society. I tried to put up a chain link and they said no way. Had to be something in keeping with the age of the home, they said. A fence like that is too rich for my blood, and for most people on this street. So we try to be good neighbors even without good fences. You know the saying?"

She nodded. "So that's what you meant about Amara not being neighborly?"

"Yup." He leaned the hoe against the side of the shed and resumed his weeding by hand, pulling plants from between the lilac's roots where the hoe couldn't reach. Bethany watched him for a few seconds, puzzled as to why he disliked the little flowers so much. They were pretty, lacy plants, and their purple-pink hue complemented the lilac bush's green, heart-shaped leaves, but he was ruthlessly yanking them out by the roots, tossing the limp plants into a pile beside him.

"So we know what you have against Amara, but what do you have against pretty flowers?" She hoped that lightening the mood would smooth over any residual resentment between the neighbors.

George picked up a handful of the plants he'd removed. "These Herb Robert? They may look nice, but they're a nuisance. Take over everything. And get a whiff—there's a reason they call it Stinking Bob." He held out the flowers to Bethany, and even without bending her head down, she caught the overwhelming and familiar scent she'd noticed before.

"Ugh! It smells like burning tires!" She waved her hand in front of her nose, and George tossed the plants on the ground, laughing.

"Here, sniff this to get it out of your nose." He bent a lilac branch toward her and she inhaled the sweet perfume of the starry blossoms. He let go of the branch and it sprang back into position just as a light breeze picked up, sending ash swirling around the yard next door.

"Shame," George murmured as he watched the windblown ashes. "Amara's place, I mean. Stood there a couple hundred years, and then gone in one night."

"Yeah—two decades of Amara's life up in smoke. Do you have any idea who might want to do something like that? Seems like a pretty serious grudge."

George chewed the inside of his lip contemplatively. "Hm. If I had to hazard a guess, I'd say it's those developer folks who have been hanging around. The ones who bought the old church down the street."

A zap of recognition buzzed through Bethany's body. *He's talking about Todd's project—the condo development!* The hair on the back of her neck stood up. "What in the world would they have against Amara?"

"Oh, not against her personally—against all of us. They've been hounding everyone to take a vote so they can go ahead and knock that old church down."

"I heard the city approved it already." *Saw the papers with my own eyes, even.*

"Yup."

Bethany's forehead furrowed. "I don't follow. Why did they need neighborhood votes if it was up to the city council?"

"You know, all the silly rules. You can build that, you can't build that, you need a proper fence. They couldn't just knock the church down because it's part of town history, see? But if enough of the neighborhood agreed, they could remove the historic designation and do whatever they wanted."

Bethany nodded. "I see. The historic status of the neighborhood meant that the church was tied up in all that bureaucracy. The developers would have to preserve the historic integrity of the building instead of knocking it down to build something new."

"Yup. But now there's no need—the fire solved that problem. One less house on the street is historic, so the whole neighborhood lost its status automatically. It's got to be a certain percent, see?"

Bethany felt the blood drain from her face, and her hands were suddenly cold. "So the condo development was only approved because of the fire?"

"Yup. Those developers are like ol' Stinking Bob, here. Their condo building will look real nice, but then they'll take over everything. Choke out all the other plants. And it stinks."

She swallowed her nausea. She'd celebrated with Todd last night—drank a champagne toast, even!—and what she had celebrated was Amara's devastating loss. She'd even been hired to cook for the groundbreaking party! *Can I even do it? Can I stomach building my career on the destruction of my best friend's childhood home?*

She watched Kimmy load the last box into the car as Amara and Sharky wedged themselves in the front seat. Amara beckoned to her through the window. *Time to go.*

"Thanks for your help, Mr. Washington."

He grunted in reply, already back at work on his flowerbeds. Bethany cut back across the lawn to the car. As she picked her way around Amara's sooty belongings, she wondered whether she should just tell Todd that she wouldn't cater the party after all. It just seemed gross to party when Amara and Kimmy were grieving all the memories they'd lost with the house. Worse than that, someone involved with the project might have been responsible—and might even attend the groundbreaking party!

She swung into the back seat and slammed the door. Even inside the vehicle, the smell of smoke clung to her, making her eyes water. She squeezed them shut as the car pulled away from the curb. *I will not serve hors d'oeuvres to the arsonist. I just won't!*

Chapter 7

Tuesday

Bethany glanced at the time as she clocked in and sucked the air between her teeth. *Late again—really late.* But hey, at least she wasn't wearing pajamas.

She looked over her shoulder as she slipped her apron on over her head and tucked her hair into a net. No sign of Alex. The door to his office was shut and she could hear male voices inside. *Lucky me—he's in a meeting.*

Maybe she wouldn't have to talk to him at all today if she slipped out quietly at the end of her shift. Then she'd walk over to Todd's office and tell him that he needed to find another caterer. He'd have to understand once he heard about her personal connection to the fire. She could audition her food for his investor another time.

She mixed a batch of batter according to the Seafood Grotto recipe. It was a classic combination of flour, milk, baking powder, salt...safe, but bland. No one was watching, so she added some garlic powder to the mixture—it didn't add any color to the batter, so Alex would never know, but it'd add some much-needed flavor!

The first lunch order came in: a three-piece cod basket. She set the potatoes to fry and battered the fresh Atlantic cod fillets, dipping them first into lemon juice—another deviation from the Seafood Grotto manual—before dredging in flour and dipping into the garlicky batter.

Her little tweaks paid off. Compliments from customers rained into the kitchen during the whole lunch shift. She clocked out feeling proud and satisfied—she'd made great food and managed to avoid getting chewed out about her punctuality problem, too! But as she turned to go out the back door, she caught a glimpse of Alex coming out of his office with a guy in a suit who looked familiar.

She racked her brain for a few seconds, trying to place him—it was Todd's investor, Don Hefferman! She ducked quickly into a storage room before Alex or Don spotted her. The last thing she needed was to get scolded—or fired!—in front of Don. He could be the key to her career move, but not if he knew she was just a fry cook at a fish and chips place!

The two men were still talking at the back door, and though she couldn't hear the content of their conversation, the tone wasn't friendly. Alex sounded just as upset with Don as he'd been with Bethany yesterday. No way she wanted to run into him now. She'd have to sneak out the front door to avoid him.

She peeked around the corner and, when Alex looked away, darted down the hall into the dining room. She let out a sigh of relief as she neared the exit, pausing only to hold the door for a customer entering the restaurant. The woman couldn't open the door herself because she was lugging an enormous antique accordion camera. Bethany couldn't help staring.

The woman looked back at her through tiny round sunglasses with wire frames, and her annoyance was unmistakable. "Close your mouth! You look like one of the codfish they serve here. You know, it's bad manners to stare."

Bethany blushed. "Sorry. I was just wondering—are you Fancy Peters?"

The woman set the camera down on an empty table and took off her sunglasses. Behind them, her pale skin glistened under the fluorescent lights of the restaurant. She nodded slowly as she scrutinized Bethany. "I am. How did you know?"

Bethany gestured to the high-necked blouse, button boots, and bicycle bloomers Fancy had on. "I heard you only wear clothes that are at least a hundred years old. Not many people fit that description."

"Hmph. Who told you that about me?"

"Amara Caldwell. Well, her niece Kimmy did."

Fancy pursed her lips and fingered the floral brooch pinned to her blouse. "Oh, them. Well, they're wrong. These are antique styles, but they're newly made. Most clothes that old can't stand up to the rigors of daily wear, and I'd hate to ruin something that had lasted a whole century. Something that old should be in a museum. Your friends need to get their facts straight."

"Well, here's a fact I have straight. You were at Amara's house on Sunday, weren't you?"

"I was there on historical society business. Hosanna Street is a very important neighborhood for Newbridge. Did you know—"

Bethany cut her off before she could launch into a lecture on local history. "Did you know that her house burned down on Sunday night—right after you visited her?"

Fancy paled. "I didn't! What a terrible loss."

Bethany couldn't believe her ears. Of course Fancy knew about the arson! There was no way she hadn't heard about the church project being approved. The historical society was the main opponent to the development and the only reason the approval went through was because of the fire. The society had to be up in arms! *So why was Fancy lying?* "You haven't read about it in the paper or anything?"

Fancy shook her head.

"I'm surprised you don't follow the happenings in such an *important* historic neighborhood."

"I mean, I heard about a fire—I just didn't realize it was Amara Caldwell's house," Fancy stammered. "I didn't pay much attention."

"You weren't curious about it? Seems like if someone is burning down historic homes, it might concern the historical society." The bells on the restaurant door jangled, and Bethany stepped aside to let another customer enter.

Fancy shook her head. "My photography has kept me busy. Anyway, if Amara Caldwell's house burned down, she probably set the fire herself."

Bethany rolled her eyes. "What? Why would she do that? She lost everything."

"But she'll get a payday, won't she? Collect the insurance money? Amara doesn't care two figs about anything except making an extra buck. She even took those developers' dirty money to build that ridiculous porch. It was a blight on Hosanna Street. Whoever lit the wick on that swan did the city a favor."

Bethany paused as she took in the new information. The *developers* had funded Amara's porch addition? Why in the world would Todd and Don give money to Amara for home improvements?

Maybe they wanted to build goodwill for their project. That could explain why Amara felt friendlier toward them than her neighbor George. Something bugged Bethany about this explanation, though.

"Why would Amara build a new porch just to burn it down?"

"Greed," Fancy Peters hissed. "Pure greed. Everyone's in it for the money. The developers bribe people to remove historic character on the street so they can build their little rathole condos for start-up millionaires. The city approves the building permits, no questions asked, because the home value goes up and they can raise the property taxes. And once her house is reappraised, your friend Amara gets a bigger payout from her insurance company if the place goes up in smoke." By the end of her little diatribe, Fancy's cheeks were flushed and her eyes were glittering.

Bethany's blood chilled. It all sounded...possible. Not crazy at all, actually. Todd was definitely ambitious enough to offer bribes to get his way, and it was likely that his friends on the city council preferred to gentrify the Hosanna Street neighborhood to generate more tax revenue for city schools and parks. Maybe Amara wasn't as innocent as she pretended, either. Maybe she'd realized the developer's bribe was a way to cash out and leave a neighborhood that didn't seem to sorry to see her go, anyway.

"How do you know all this? What proof do you have?"

Fancy tapped her camera. "I document everything. I spend plenty of time on Hosanna Street, and I've seen them together. Amara Caldwell rubbing elbows with the developers. Developers kissing up to the mayor and city council. All plotting to destroy Newbridge for their own gain."

Bethany realized with a jolt that all the people in question—the developers, the city council and mayor, the tech millionaires—all of them would be at the groundbreaking gala. Maybe instead of backing out, she should cater the party and ask some questions. If she could find out more about Amara's relationship with the developers and the developers' relationships with city officials, she just might figure out who burned down the house on Hosanna Street.

Fancy broke the silence. "Come by the souvenir shop in the train station sometime if you don't believe me. I'll show you the negatives."

Bethany nodded. "I believe you."

Fancy looked gleeful, and something about her wild expression made Bethany's skin crawl. Revulsion must have shown on her face, because Fancy leaned toward her and spoke softly. "Everybody's out for something in this town. Mind your own business so you don't get burned."

Bethany took a step back and bumped into someone behind her. "Sorry," she said automatically.

"You better be," Alex Vadecki growled. "Are you bothering customers now?"

Bethany sighed. Of course it was Alex, the one person she was trying to avoid. "No, I'm just leaving."

"I'm really sorry you were disrupted by an employee, ma'am," he said to Fancy. "Your meal is on the house."

"I wasn't bothering her!" Bethany crossed her arms as Fancy scooped up her camera and went to order at the counter. "We were just talking."

Alex grunted. "Just what I need: bad press." He opened the door for her and pointed to the sidewalk. "Out!"

Bethany rolled her eyes and stepped outside. "Press?"

Alex followed her out and closed the door behind him. "I know that lady. She sells her pictures to the paper sometimes. Or she turns them into postcards and sells them as Newbridge souvenirs. I don't want her getting the wrong idea about the restaurant from you! Not when I'm this close to sealing the deal."

Bethany frowned. *The deal?* Was that why Alex was meeting with Don Hefferman—a restaurant investment? She hadn't realized Don was talking to other restauranteurs, but now that she thought about it, of course he was. She really couldn't miss the groundbreaking now, not if she wanted a chance at partnering with Don. Not if she was competing with seasoned restaurateurs like Alex Vadecki. He seemed lost in thought, chewing his lip and staring at the brick wall behind her.

"Can I ask you a favor?" Bethany asked meekly.

Alex rubbed his forehead. "What now?"

"You know I've been dating that real estate guy, Todd? Well, he asked me to cater a party for him tomorrow, and I was wondering if maybe I could do the prep here at the Grotto. It wouldn't be until after closing time. And I'll do all the cleanup—you won't even know I was here." She smiled, trying to look cute and cheerful, but it came out more of a grimace as she braced herself for his reply.

"Is that the groundbreaking party for the new condo development?"

She nodded.

"Absolutely not. I'm attending that party, and I'm not interested in having my business associated with your amateur hour."

That stings. "I'll be catering the party whether you let me cook here or not," she said coolly, even though she was burning with indignation on the inside. "I guess I'll see you there."

He pointed a finger at her and narrowed his eyes. "Don't you dare mention my name or my restaurant. I don't want you using your connection to my business to promote yourself. If you do, you can kiss your job goodbye."

Chapter 8

"**Y**ou have an appointment?" Todd's administrative assistant looked over the top of her turquoise glasses and sized up Bethany. Then she scanned the desk calendar in front of her, sliding a matching turquoise fingernail down the daily schedule. "I don't see you here."

Bethany grit her teeth. Her stomach was already roiling from her argument with Alex, and this lady wasn't helping it settle. But she didn't want to come off like a crazy girlfriend, either, demanding to be let into Todd's office just because they'd gone on a few dates.

"Um, I'm catering the party tomorrow?"

"Oh, sure." The admin assistant tapped her nails on the calendar as if rendering a final judgment. "I'll let him know you're here."

"Thanks so much." It was everything Bethany could do to keep the sarcasm out of her voice. *Glad I passed muster.*

A few minutes later, Todd emerged and held out hand to her. "Come in, come in! Did Shirley give you a hard time?"

Shirley shot Bethany a *look*, and Bethany shook her head. "No, it's fine."

"She's just doing her job. I need a pitbull on the front desk." *Of course, he didn't tell her that I'm his girlfriend.*

"Wouldn't want just anybody slipping in." Bethany smiled sweetly as they walked down the hall, but the fake smile made her cheeks felt like they were going to crack. She slid into one of the guest chairs in Todd's sleek, gray office and slumped in the seat.

Instead of going behind the desk, he sat down beside her. "What's up? You look terrible!"

"Gee, thanks." She sat up straighter and smoothed the fly-aways into her bun, suddenly conscious that she'd just come from a grueling shift. She probably stank like fried fish! *No wonder the front desk lady was so hesitant to let me in.*

He put his arm around her and leaned in for a hug. "You know what I mean. You usually have a smile on your face. Was Shirley really that bad?"

"Nah." She sighed. "It's just my boss. We had a fight at the end of my shift because I was talking to a customer. Fancy Peters. I assume you know her? She's probably all up in your business about the development."

Todd nodded and loosened his necktie a little. "Historical society? Yeah." He cleared his throat. "Why'd you happen to talk to her?"

Nervous about something, Todd? She shrugged. "I just thought she might have seen something related to the arson on Hosanna Street. She was there that night."

Todd stood up and walked to the window, then pulled up the blinds so he could stare out into the distance. His view from the fifth floor of the office building was almost as good as the view from Bethany's cottage. "You can see it from here. The development, I mean." He pointed to the northeast, where the bell tower of the historic church was just visible above the leafy treetops. "See?"

"Mhm." What she didn't see was Amara Caldwell's house. She should have had a view of that, too, but it was gone, and the thought made her heart squeeze. She crossed the room to stand behind Todd and gazed out the window over his shoulder. "Did you really give Kimmy's aunt the money to build her swan porch addition?"

Todd glanced over his shoulder and rushed to shut the office door. "Shh! Not so loud! Did Fancy Peters tell you that?"

"Who cares who told me! Did you or didn't you?" She put her hands on her hips and glared at him. *Lie to my face, Todd—I dare you.*

He sighed sheepishly as he looked out the window toward the church again. "I might have given some cash to people on Hosanna Street so they could afford improvements. Just so they could spiff up their exteriors a little."

Bethany took a deep breath. *Reserve judgment. Don't jump to conclusions. He might have a valid explanation.* She closed her eyes for a second as she waited a beat to calm her voice and then opened them again. "I guess I don't understand why you did that."

"It's part of my job!" Todd flashed his teeth at her, the same fake smile that he wore in the headshots on his shiny new website. "I don't expect you to understand the ins and outs of real estate development, hon."

A little condescension isn't going to derail me, mister. Bethany fake-smiled back at him, gritting her teeth. In a syrupy-sweet voice, she asked, "Maybe you could explain it to me?"

"Let me see if I can put this in terms that will make sense to you." He sat down in his desk chair and spun around. "You can take a piece of fish, right? And sell it for five bucks. Or you can dress it up with...I don't know, parsley or something? And sell it for fifteen bucks. Follow me?"

Yes, because I'm not an idiot, Todd.

"Well, basically, if you serve five dollar fish, the fifteen-dollar customers won't come to that restaurant. They want the parsley. Get it?"

She nodded, even though she wanted to say that a parsley garnish would add two bucks to the price of the fish, not ten. "You think you can charge more for your condos if the houses on the street look nicer?"

"You were paying attention!" Todd gave her a thumbs up, and Bethany wanted to scream.

"So it wasn't to decrease the historic value of the neighborhood and fast-track your development project?" She used the same syrupy-sweet voice as before, a sugary blade. Her words had their intended effect—his cheeks flushed and his sleazy smile vanished.

"They didn't have to take the money." He tipped back in his chair and propped his shiny loafers on the desk. The soles were surprisingly clean even though the heels were worn. Leave it to Todd to wash the bottoms of his shoes. "It's not my fault if they didn't do their due diligence and get the projects approved by the historical society."

"Convenient for you. They accidentally skip the bureaucracy and suddenly you get to skip it, too. You knew they wouldn't go through the proper channels!"

Todd turned the charm back on. "Come on, Bethy. How could I know that?"

She stamped her foot. "Because most of the people who live on Hosanna Street are older! They aren't up on all the rules and regulations—they just want to live in the neighborhood where they raised their kids and their families have lived for generations!"

Todd chuckled. "They'll be crying all the way to the bank when their property values skyrocket because of my development. Let it go, kiddo. This is a win-win."

Let it go?! She didn't think so. Hands on her hips, she asked, "Was the arson a win? Because it seems like it paved the way for instant approval of the development. Now my friends' lives are destroyed, and you're going to be a big guy, rubbing elbows with the muckety mucks of Newbridge at the party! But I mean, who cares about Amara's little house when you get to hang out with the mayor, right?"

He waved his hand. "Just an ugly coincidence."

She narrowed her eyes. "If the fire is just a coincidence, then I'm surprised you're not concerned about an arsonist loose on Hosanna Street. Doesn't seem like that will exactly make property values skyrocket. I doubt anyone will want to move into a new condo if they're afraid to go to sleep at night, either."

"Don't talk like that!" He frowned at her, his mask of charm and professionalism falling away. "Especially not at the party. Negative publicity could ruin the chances of the condo project finding good tenants. If people start associating the neighborhood with criminal activity, that'll be the end."

Bethany snorted derisively. "Heaven forbid you don't instantly make millions of dollars. Then you might have to be a regular person like me."

"Are you jealous of my success? Maybe I should get someone else to cater the gala. Someone who *wants* me to succeed." His eyes welled up, and he blinked furiously. "I'm just trying to help you, Bethy, like I was trying to help out the people on Hosanna Street. I thought I was being a good neighbor. I didn't think anyone would get hurt."

Did he really think she'd feel sorry for him when he was so callous about the fire?! Bethany threw up her hands. "If you really want to be a good neighbor, then you should be marginally invested in who did this! Come on!"

He pinched the bridge of his nose and grimaced. "I am, I am. Don't get the wrong idea. I'll ask around the office and see if anyone knows anything. Maybe they saw something when they were in the neighborhood that afternoon."

"You were in the neighborhood then, right?"

Todd stood up abruptly and frowned. "I don't remember. Maybe. I go up to Hosanna Street a lot."

"Did you see anyone hanging around Amara's house?"

Todd shrugged. "I don't know if it was Saturday or Sunday, but the last time I remember going by Amara's, her neighbor—old guy, maybe eighty?—was outside mowing the yard. Kept glaring over his shoulder at her place like it had spit in his coffee or something. I tried to talk to him, but he just ignored me and kept mowing."

"Must have been George," Bethany said, remembering her conversation with him earlier. What had he called the condo developers? *Oh yeah, Stinking Bob, the weed that looked pretty but took over everything around it.*

"That's right. George Washington. Not a name you forget easily. He's one of the ones who doesn't really like us being in the neighborhood. We try to butter those people up, but he didn't want any part of it. We're inviting the whole street to the gala tomorrow, though. A little wining and dining and they'll see we're not so bad. Your food will win them over." Todd smiled at her awkwardly.

"Should we talk menu?" she asked.

He shook his head. "I trust you! You're a superstar in the kitchen. I know you won't let me down—you want this as much as I do."

"Right. But like how many people, sit down or buffet, theme, stuff like that?"

He ticked off on his fingers. "Between the historical society, the city council, the neighborhood residents...I think three, four."

She gaped at him. "Hundred?"

"Yeah, hundred. Not three or four people. Come on, Bethany. This is a big deal."

"I know, I know." Her brain was buzzing. She'd expected a more manageable number—sixty or seventy, tops. "How am I supposed to prep for and serve that many people all by myself?"

"How everyone else does. Hire someone! Sheesh." Todd shook his head and slid open the desk drawer. He got out a check book and waited, pen poised over it. "How much do you need?"

"I don't even know. I have to totally rethink how to approach this!" Her voice rose a little at the end, panic seeping into her words. *Professionalism. Stay calm. This is just like a real catering gig.* She took a deep breath before she continued, keeping her voice level. "I'll put everything on a credit card and you can reimburse me afterward. I know you're good for it."

Todd's shoulders relaxed and he grinned broadly at her as he shut the checkbook back in the desk drawer. "That's my girl.

You got this. Don's going to be so impressed with you. Heck, the whole town is going to know both our names after this event!"

Despite the panic still surging through her veins, Bethany couldn't help cracking a smile at that idea. "I hope so. Don't forget to ask around about Amara's house, OK?"

"What?" A blank look replaced his grin.

"If anyone saw anything on Sunday," she reminded him.

"Oh, yeah. Will do." Todd stared out the window in the direction of Hosanna Street, barely glancing her way to say goodbye. He must be as stressed about the event as she was.

As she walked down the hall, past Sylvia, and toward the exit, she gave herself a mental pep talk. *I can do this. I can do this. Three hundred people. Four hundred hungry people. Big investor. Tomorrow.*

Her stomach knotted as she strode out of the building toward the bus stop. She'd head home, plan the menu, and wait for Kimmy to come home from her shift at Café Sabine. She would know what to do, and the only way Bethany was going to get through this was if she called on every friend she had.

Chapter 9

"OK, I got you three of my part-time waiters to pass apps." Kimmy put down her phone and propped her elbows on the kitchen table. "It isn't a full staff for an event that size, but you can have a buffet-style setup so people can help themselves, too. Plus that'll draw them to you, and you'll get to make some connections, hopefully."

Bethany felt some of the weight fall away from her shoulders. "You're so good to me. I'm so sorry to bug you about this and keep you up late when you are dealing with so much." She looked over at the sofa where Kimmy's great-aunt was snoring lightly, her head tilted back and her arms crossed. Sharky perched on her abdomen, chewing on a ham bone Kimmy had brought home from the café. The little dog rose and fell with every breath Amara took.

"It's no trouble." Kimmy's eyes were tired, though, and Bethany knew it was a strain. "What are you going to make?"

"I'm thinking something summery and easy to eat without utensils, so we can skip renting silverware. And not too many dishes so I have time to execute."

"Smart."

Bethany scanned the notes she'd made on her phone. "What do you think of corn chowder?"

Kimmy looked thoughtful. "Maybe playing it a little safe? Plus you'd need a spoon to eat it."

"Well, I could serve it in a shot glass. I'll add a drop of basil oil to make it interesting. And then a little grilled veggie skewer—I can rent a grill and cook them on-site—and cherrystone clams on the half shell. They're in season, and my guy Jim down at the fish market will shuck them and make platters on ice for me. And Todd is taking care of the champagne so I'll just have some lemon-cucumber water to drink."

"Yum! That all sounds amazing!" Kimmy said.

"I just need to talk Alex into letting me make the soup at the Seafood Grotto. I don't know if he's going to go for it. If he doesn't, I'll grill something instead of making the chowder."

"If all you need to do is the soup, I can totally squeeze you in at the café. I'll be prepping for dinner service at the same time, but I can clear a counter and a burner for you."

"Would you? Won't your boss mind?"

"Monsieur Adrian's in France sourcing cheese right now, so he doesn't even have to know." Kimmy still looked tired, but her eyes twinkled mischievously. "Speaking of cheese, I brought home some leftover chèvre and honey tarts. Want one?"

Bethany giggled. "Have I ever turned down a dessert? Did you make them?"

Kimmy shook her head. "Ordered from the Honor Roll. Olive is such a good baker that I don't even bother trying anymore. Almost all our desserts come from her." She started to stand up, but Bethany waved her back into her seat.

"Don't even think about it. After all you've done for me tonight, the least I can do is get out the tarts."

Late-night snacking was kind of their thing. It started out as a way to reward themselves after a tough exam in culinary school, and had morphed into one of Bethany's favorite routines. Every night after work, they'd share dessert or special drinks and catch up on the day. Sometimes it was after midnight when Kimmy got home, but they always took a few minutes to connect.

As Bethany reached into the fridge to pull out the foilwrapped tarts, a sleepy voice from the sofa drawled, "I dearly hope there's one in there for me."

"Yep, she brought three," Bethany called over her shoulder. "You woke up just in time."

Amara sat up, dislodging Sharky's ham bone from her lap, and the dog jumped to the floor to grab it. Amara slid into a seat at the table and stifled a yawn. "I wasn't sleeping."

"Of course not." Kimmy shared a bemused look with Bethany. "We must have imagined those snores."

"I heard everything you said. Bethany, child, if you're going to barbecue, you know you won't be able to serve that other stuff at the same time. I better come along."

Maybe Amara *had* heard everything they'd said. Bethany nodded and set a small dessert plate down in front of her. "You're right. I need more help at the main table. But I can't let you do that! Not when this party is happening because...well. It's not right. I'll find someone else. Maybe one of our classmates from culinary school."

Amara stabbed the tart with her fork. "Nonsense. This way I'll repay your hospitality. Besides, I was the outdoor cooking champion of Orleans Parish when I was a girl. I can out-grill anybody from your fancy school."

"Is that even a real thing, Auntie?"

"Of course it's real! Nineteen forty-nine. You can look it up on your gadgety-goo." Amara motioned with her fork to Kimmy's phone. "All my friends from the neighborhood will be there anyway. Maybe they'll have some ideas about who lit fire to my beautiful home. You know how fast news travels on Hosanna Street."

Kimmy nodded. "It's not a very big neighborhood, and everyone's pretty close."

"Well, I can't say no to that." Bethany looked back and forth between the two women. She'd never really thought that Kimmy was much like Amara, but she could see more similarities now. Both were loyal and generous, maybe to a fault. "The grilling will mostly be at the beginning, so you should have time to find out what your friends know about the arson. And if your friends don't know, maybe one of Todd's people do. Somebody at this gala has to know something."

Kimmy straightened up in her chair and spoke through a mouthful of tart. "You think maybe you can figure it out at the event?"

"Oh honey, I am going to get to the bottom of it, I'm telling you." Amara dusted crumbs from the front of her bronze silk caftan. Sharky left the splintered remains of his bone on the sofa and darted underneath her chair, where he gobbled the crumbs from the floor. When he'd vacuumed them all up, he stood on his hind legs and bounced up and down, begging for more.

As Bethany watched Amara fuss over the dog, she wondered if it was a mistake accepting Amara's offer to help. This menu was perfect, exactly the kind of fresh, casual, seasonal food she dreamed of serving at her future restaurant. If Amara offended Don by grilling him figuratively while she grilled the vegetables literally, Bethany's chance at owning her own place would go down the tubes.

But on the flip side, Amara couldn't live here forever, either. The woman deserved answers to who set her house on fire so she could collect the insurance money and move on. *Assuming, of course, that Amara hadn't set it on fire herself, whether by accident or on purpose.*

"Just out of curiosity, why did you build the porch addition?" Bethany asked as she cleared the dessert plates from the table.

Amara propped her elbows on the table and surveyed its worn top as though she were looking at a spread of tarot cards. "I suppose it reminds me of my growing up years down south. Every house had a screen porch. You had to have one to enjoy yourself in the summertime. People would have a screen porch before they'd have a car or even a telephone, it was that much of a necessity. I don't understand why it isn't the same up here. The mosquitos are just as big and just as nasty."

"Plus you had that swan from the carousel just sitting in a shed," Kimmy added. "You've always wanted it to see the light of day."

No mention about the developers funding the project. Why was Amara omitting that detail? "Seems like an expensive project."

"It wasn't too dear. I scraped it together." Amara picked up Sharky and nuzzled him, avoiding Bethany's attempts at eye contact.

Maybe she's embarrassed that she took Todd's bribe. Bethany rinsed the dishes and stacked them in the dish drainer as she debated whether or not to push the issue. On one hand, she really wanted answers. If Amara had been planning this porch addition for a long time, then maybe she just took advantage of an opportunity when the developers came with their check-book.

But if she hadn't been planning this swan porch, maybe it was what Fancy Peters claimed—maybe Amara took their free money and built the addition so she could burn it down later and collect the insurance payout on a house with a higher value.

She dried her hands on a dish towel and sat back down at the table where Kimmy and Amara were still chatting. When their conversation paused, she asked, "How long did you save up for the addition?"

The instant the words were out of her mouth, she regretted it. Kimmy looked at her with an eyebrow raised. She clearly thought that the answer—whatever it might be—was none of Bethany's beeswax.

Bethany felt her cheeks flush. She fumbled for the right words. "I mean...have you been planning it for a while? I just wondered about the timing."

"I wanted the porch to be done for the summer," Amara said coolly. "So I could sit outside without being eaten alive." Her face was smooth and placid, but Bethany could hear an undercurrent of anger in her voice.

Great. Just what I need—two roommates upset with me. As usual, her suspicious nature was making her enemies. She needed to smooth things over before there was a full mutiny and Kimmy bailed on letting her use the kitchen tomorrow. "Makes sense. I bet that didn't sit well with Fancy Peters, did it?"

Amara laughed, and the tension in the room broke. "That woman wanted me to go through their whole historical society rigmarole. She came to my house every blessed day with paperwork to fill out. I said no thank you, it's my house and I'm not waiting until you people say it's all right. By then it'll be too late and I won't be able to enjoy my porch until next summer. I'm not a young woman, I told her. I can't wait a year."

"Weren't you worried there would be some consequence for not following the rules?"

Amara snorted. "Those rules were just made up by some white ladies so they could tell us how to live. Black folks have been taking care of Hosanna Street since it was built, haven't we? That's why it's historic. The society doesn't own it just because it's old—we own it. They can go boss their own neighborhood."

"She has a point," Kimmy said. "Hosanna Street was built by free African-Americans back when most were still enslaved, and for a long time it was considered the wrong side of the tracks, literally. The historical society only cares about the neighborhood now because it's old and well-maintained—it was never demolished to build office buildings or whatever because nobody thought it was worth investing here."

"Of course I have a point!" Amara sniffed. "Besides, I looked it up, and the historical society doesn't have any legal legs to stand on. They can't even impose a fine. All they can do is vote my house off the historic registry, and then I can paint it any color I want. I can turn it into a hot air balloon if I choose. But I knew they wouldn't do that, because the street wouldn't have enough historic buildings to be a historic neighborhood, and the developers would get their way, anyway. So Fancy Peters had to put up with my swan porch."

"If she penalized you for it, the historical society would lose their battle with the condo developers. So you took the developers' money because you thought it was a chance to build your porch without the society coming down too hard on you?" Bethany clapped her hand over her mouth—she hadn't meant to let it slip that she knew Amara had taken money from Todd's company.

"That's right."

Kimmy's head swiveled toward Bethany and then back to Amara. "What do you mean, the developers' money?!"

Now Amara avoided eye contact with Kimmy. "They were going around writing checks to people for home improvements. No reason why I shouldn't get mine, too."

Kimmy pushed her chair back and stood up. "Your boyfriend was doing this?! Why?"

Bethany bit her lip. "I didn't know, Kimmy. I asked him about it after Fancy Peters told me, and he said it was to fix up the neighborhood so the property values would rise, and then he'd be able to get better buyers for his condos. But honestly, I think it might be because he was hoping the historical society would crack down and kick some homes off the registry. The condo development was not going to be approved unless that happened."

"They tried to buy some places, too. Tried all kinds of things. They thought we were stupid." Amara scratched Sharky under the chin. "But we aren't stupid, are we? No, we aren't. We played their game, but we won."

"But you didn't win, Auntie," Kimmy said in a small voice. "Someone made sure of that."

Chapter 10

Wednesday

Bethany pried herself out of bed at the crack of dawn, relying on coffee and sheer will to pedal to the growers' market to buy produce and then down to the marina to order the clam shooters. She managed to deliver the vegetables to Café Sabine, where Kimmy kindly opened the door early for her, and make it to the Seafood Grotto with about seven seconds to spare before her shift started.

She had just dropped the basket on her second order of fried oysters when Alex wandered into the kitchen. Out of the corner of her eye, she saw him peer over the shoulders of other cooks on the line, checking their work one-by-one, until he got to her station at the fryer. There he stopped, breathing on the back of her neck as she jiggled the basket so the oysters wouldn't stick together.

"What?!" she finally snapped, when she couldn't stand it anymore. She pulled the basket out of the fryer and nabbed the oysters out with her tongs. They were perfectly done. "Sorry. You're just freaking me out standing there."

Alex took a step back. "I was just going to say that you're doing a great job on those oysters. They look awesome." He smiled at her.

Bethany frowned. Why was he being so weirdly nice? He never gave compliments.

"Come on; let's have a chat." Alex smiled again, which looked out of place on his face—he literally had never smiled at her before—and headed for his office.

He's definitely going to fire me. Why else would he act so nice? She sighed and called to one of the other cooks to cover her station.

She closed the door behind her and took a seat across from him. He looked down at a piece of paper on his desk and cleared his throat. *Here it comes, the "we have to let you go" script.*

"You're really an asset to the business. I want you to know that."

She groaned internally. She'd have to put up with more compliments before he had the courage to deliver the bad news. "If you really thought that, you'd listen to me more."

"What do you mean?" He looked genuinely taken aback.

"Well, like when I offer easy improvements to recipes, you don't even consider it."

He sighed. "I do consider it, but I have to factor in cost. If I change the cost of an order, it throws everything out of whack. Even if it's just a penny's worth of garlic powder."

Bethany cringed. He must have noticed her tweak to the fish batter recipe the other day, even though he hadn't said anything about it. "Couldn't you just adjust portion size or add a couple cents to the price the customer pays? Doesn't seem like a huge deal."

"It's not." He rolled his eyes, exasperated. "I mean, it wouldn't be, but—this is why I called you in here."

She rolled her eyes. "Why's that?" she asked, although she was already pretty sure of the answer. *Things are tight, can't afford a staff this size, blah blah blah—spit it out, man!*

"I'm franchising the Seafood Grotto. I put together a whole franchise package, and that includes a set menu, food costs, décor, everything. There'll be Grottos up and down the coast soon!"

"So that's why you're so obsessed with consistent mediocrity."

"Yes. I mean, no. I'm going to pretend you didn't say that, because I can't get mad at you right now. I need you on board for the meeting." He tapped the paper in front of him.

"What meeting?" Bethany craned her neck to read the paper on Alex's desk upside down, but couldn't make out what it said. "I'm confused. Are you firing me?"

His face turned red. "What? No! I need you to be the demo cook for the meeting with my franchise investor. I want to show him the full menu, and you're the best cook on staff."

She was pleasantly surprised to hear the words *you're the best* come out of his mouth. "OK, sure. When is it?"

"After close this afternoon, four o'clock. I'll pay overtime."

"Oh, I can't! I'm catering the gala, remember?"

His face turned an even deeper shade of red. "I told you not to take that gig, didn't I?! This is important! Way more important than playing at being a caterer for your boyfriend's party. I swear, if you can't come through for me on this, I will make sure you never have a restaurant career in Newbridge!" By the end of his tirade, he was shouting. He seemed to realize that he'd stepped over the line and pressed the back of his hand to his mouth, his chest heaving.

"I'm sorry, Alex. I really am—but I already committed. I can't back out now. Can't you move the demo to tomorrow?"

"I can't, genius, or I would have. Tonight's the night. If the Grotto can't perform, the investor is out—and so are you. If you're so committed to catering, fine. Kiss your job goodbye. I'm done with you."

Chapter 11

Wednesday

Sylvia brought a second box of Kleenex into Todd's office and gave Bethany a sympathetic look as she closed the door behind her.

"Look on the bright side, Bethy," Todd said, squeezing her shoulder. "Now I can tell people I'm dating someone who owns their own catering business."

Yeah, instead of lying to them about what I do, Bethany thought darkly. She snuffled and dabbed her nose with a tissue. "Alex said he's going to sabotage me. He said I won't be able to get another job in Newbridge."

Todd rolled his eyes. "You don't need a job! You're self-employed now."

She hiccupped. "Getting hired by my boyfriend for one gig isn't exactly a career. It's not easy to get catering jobs without a ton of connections and experience."

"Now who's sabotaging you?" Todd prodded her shoulder again. "You are. Tonight, you're going to make all kinds of connections with important people and add some experience to your resume, too. And I'm sure we'll use you again to cater our events, too. We're going to have a lot to celebrate around here. Everyone's excited to bring Hosanna Street into the twenty-first century!"

She raised her head. "Speaking of Hosanna Street, have you asked around about the arson? Does anyone know anything about it?"

"It's been so busy..."

"You haven't even asked?!"

"Of course I did—I said I would." He looked slightly miffed, and Bethany felt a twinge of guilt for assuming the worst. "I had one of the assistants ask around. He said someone saw a creepy old guy lurking around there on Sunday."

"Was it George Washington?"

Todd shrugged. "They didn't ask his name. They just noticed he seemed interested in her house. Kept looking over there."

Bethany rolled her eyes. "He lives next door. Where is he supposed to look? Any direction he looks, he's staring at someone's house."

Todd put up his hands defensively. "Hey, I'm not accusing the guy of anything. I wasn't even there. I've been way too busy planning the gala to play detective. This is just what someone saw, and you wanted to know about it. Don't shoot the messenger!"

The door to Todd's office swung open and Don Hefferman stuck his head in. "Hey! If it isn't Ms. Bradstreet. Sylvia said you were here. Todd's been telling me how great you are, and I can't wait to finally taste for myself."

"Don." Todd nodded at him.

Bethany stuck out her hand, hoping the last of the tears had dried on her cheeks. "Good to see you. Hope you like clams."

"Boy, do I. I've got a real thing for seafood." Don shook her hand firmly. "What else is on the menu tonight? No, wait, don't tell me. Surprise me along with the rest of the crowd."

She chuckled. "Will do. I'm sure you'll want to talk with everyone there, so stop by the table early, before the food's all gone! Actually, speaking of talking to everyone, have you heard anything about the arson on Hosanna Street? I mean, heard any rumors when you've been around the neighborhood or whatever?"

Todd shifted uncomfortably, and Don's broad smile faded a bit.

"Oh, well, I'm not really a man-on-the-street type. I leave that to this guy here." He clapped Todd on the back. "I'm just the bank account. Frankly, I haven't heard about any arson. What's she talking about?" He looked at Todd, who seemed to be very interested in rearranging items on his desk.

"Nothing to worry about, Don. Nothing to do with the condo project, just an idle question. A friend of Bethany's has a little personal situation, that's all."

"Not exactly *nothing* to do with it!" she blurted out. "It's the whole reason the project was approved!"

"Not the whole reason, Bethy." Todd used a tone of voice usually reserved for kindergarteners. "We had layers of approval, permits, planning. This project was going to happen now or six months from now, but it was going to happen. The arson—the fire—just cleared the last hurdle. But we would have gotten there anyway."

"Not with his money, though." Bethany pointed at Don, who clutched his chest as though she'd pointed a gun and fired. He sat down heavily in a chair. "He would have walked away if Amara's house hadn't been burned to the ground."

Todd whirled to face Don. "She's just blowing off steam. Don't pay any attention."

Don shook his head. "Is this true, Todd? Did the church re-development get pushed through because someone's home was destroyed?"

"Yes, but it doesn't change anything about our partnership. One way or another, I'm confident we'd have built the Hosanna Street condos." He smiled, whitened teeth flashing, but the smile didn't reach his eyes.

"I'm not so sure," Don muttered, his head bowed.

"Doesn't matter now, does it? Everything's good. We're moving forward!" Todd's voice was too jovial, almost pleading, and Bethany cringed internally. "It's going to be Newbridge's first luxury development. The waiting list for condos will be a mile long."

Don raised one hand to stop Todd's rambling, the other still clutching his chest. "I was sure you would miss the deadline—so sure that I made a major investment in another business. I can't back out of either one now. I won't BS you, Todd—we're stretched very thin here. This condo project can't go a cent over budget, or we're all screwed. Bad press, bad reputation, the tiniest thing could send this development into the toilet."

"I hear you. Roger that. We'll run a tight operation. No overages, scout's honor."

Like Todd was ever a Boy Scout. She snorted, and then coughed to cover up the noise.

Don stood and it seemed to Bethany that he'd aged five years since he'd entered the office. His shoulders slumped and the lines on his forehead had deepened. "It's more than the budget. You better clean up this arson situation before it gets out of hand. If even one person"—he motioned to

Bethany—"thinks there's some truth to this thing, we might as well dissolve our partnership now."

Bethany opened her mouth to say that there *was* truth to it, but Todd shot her such a stormy look that she didn't dare say a word until he'd ushered Don out of the office with apologies and soothing promises. He returned like a hurricane, slamming the door behind him so hard that it rattled the window.

"What the *heck*, Bethany?! Why'd you have to ask him about that?"

She sighed. "I just wondered what he knew. Aren't you curious?"

Todd raked his hand through his hair so it stuck straight up in wild spikes. "No, I'm not, because he doesn't know anything. He's just the money guy, my meal ticket—and I shouldn't have to remind you that he's *your* meal ticket, too!"

"I thought he already knew about the connection. Everyone knows about the arson."

"There's no connection! It was just a terrible coincidence that has turned into a terrible rumor. And now you've weakened my relationship with my sole investor by spreading it around." Todd sat down at his desk and stared up at the ceiling, blinking furiously, and she realized that he was trying not to cry.

She shrugged. "If it's just a coincidence, then I'm sure things will be fine with Don."

Todd pounded on the desk like a toddler about to lay down an adult-size tantrum. "No, things won't be 'fine with Don.'" He mimicked her in an ugly, saccharine voice. "Don will be suspicious of any changes to the condo project now. He'll be scrutinizing every cent. He might even bail on the whole thing!

You know, it's one thing for you to sabotage your own career, and it's another thing when you try to sabotage mine!"

She leaned forward across the desk until their faces were inches apart. "For your information, I don't have a career now. I got *fired* because I agreed to cater your stupid party. So if we're going to talk about sabotage, you better look in the mirror! You're the one who coerced me to take a gig under false pretenses!"

He gasped. "What are you *talking* about? Since when was the biggest opportunity of your life a false pretense?"

"Don isn't going to invest in a restaurant! He doesn't have the money. He said himself he's stretched paper thin just with his current investments. I jeopardized my job because I thought this could be my big break, but you were just using me to get cheap catering for your event."

"It's not *that* cheap." Todd jutted out his chin. "I had no idea Don had already committed to another project. Anyway, you didn't know he was tapped out until *after* you brought up the arson, so you have no excuse for the way you tried to ruin me!"

Bethany's mouth fell open. "So you think I'd be justified in trying to ruin you if it was for revenge? What kind of person are you?!" *The kind of person who would set someone's home on fire for personal gain?* His reluctance to even casually investigate the fire, his extreme reaction to her questions for Don...why was he acting so strange? She put her hands on her hips, daring him to avoid the question. "Where were you on Sunday evening?"

He gazed sullenly at the floor. "Why does it matter?"

"You know why."

"Because you think I did it? You think I burned down Kimmy's childhood home?" He pressed his lips together and avoided eye contact, his arms crossed tightly. "If that's what you think of me, we shouldn't see each other anymore."

Her stomach knotted, not because he was breaking up with her, but because he'd used their relationship to artfully dodge the question. "Where were you on Sunday evening?" she repeated calmly.

"I didn't set that house on fire."

Her heart sank. "But you were there, weren't you?"

He stood up abruptly and walked to the window, staring out at the Hosanna Street church steeple in the distance and gnawing on his lip. "Fine. Yes, I went to Amara's house on Sunday to ask if she'd come to the city council meeting the next day to speak in favor of the condo development. She was one of our biggest allies in the neighborhood and my last hope for getting the project approved. But her house *wasn't* on fire when I left."

"Anyone see you leave? Forgive me for not taking your word for it," she said sourly.

"Besides Amara herself? I don't know. Wait, the creepy old neighbor guy I was talking about!"

"So it was you who saw him, not some nameless employee?" *Another lie...they were piling up.*

He nodded. "He was trying to push his lawnmower into a shed, but it was getting hung up on something. I helped him move it inside. I remember because I got gasoline or oil or something on my shoes and had to have them cleaned. The old guy didn't even offer to pay for it."

If she hadn't smelled the gasoline herself on Monday night, she wouldn't have believed him. But she remembered the sharp smell clearly. *He must have had a reason for helping George, an ulterior motive—maybe he wanted an alibi?*

"Since when are you the type to lend a hand to anyone if you aren't getting something out of it?"

Todd's face crumpled. "I'm just trying to build goodwill, that's all. You have to understand, on Sunday night I was pretty sure the development wouldn't be approved at the city council meeting, and I was worried Don was going to bail on the deal once we missed the deadline. I thought it couldn't hurt if another Hosanna Street neighbor had a good opinion of me, OK? Like maybe the guy would put in a good word, too. Is that so horrible?"

He looked so pitiful that she felt the teensiest bit bad for being so hard with him. Not bad enough to keep dating him, though. "It's a little horrible. Most people would help just to be nice."

He rubbed his face with both hands, and then slicked his wild hair back down into its usual perfect coif. "I guess I'm a little bit horrible then. Nice knowing you, Bethy. Don't worry about the catering tonight," he added smoothly. "I'll pick up some deli trays from Cheapko. Don will appreciate my new-found thriftiness."

He walked over to his office door and opened it so she could leave, revealing Shirley standing on the other side with a horrified look on her face. She'd clearly heard everything that had gone on inside the office.

"Sorry!" Shirley chirped, and scurried back down the hall toward her desk.

Todd jerked his head after her. "You can follow her out."

You're not getting rid of me that easily. Bethany put her hand on his arm. "Just because we broke up doesn't mean I'm backing out of our catering agreement." If Todd had something to hide, she wanted to know what it was—and the best place to find out was that gala. Plus, it was the only paycheck on the horizon now that she'd been fired from the Grotto.

He looked at her, eyebrows raised. "You're not?"

She shook her head. "No, we made a verbal contract, and I'll honor it. Anyway, I already ordered the food. What am I going to do with 1500 clams?"

"Wow, huh." For once, Todd seemed at a loss for words. "Thanks, Bethy."

She grinned. There was an upside to the end of the relationship—she didn't have to put up with that dumb nickname anymore. "Don't call me that ever again. I really hate it."

"My bad." Todd shrugged. "See you at the gala, I guess."

So much enthusiasm. So much gratitude.

On her way out of the building, Bethany couldn't help but wonder if she'd accepted his reason for the breakup too quickly. His only rationale was that she wouldn't want to be with someone as morally bankrupt as him—which was true! But surely that would be her decision, not his. *He must have a hidden reason for ending our relationship.*

Not cute enough, not ambitious enough, not successful enough. She ticked off the reasons on her fingers. But he knew all that stuff about her before, and he was still planning their power-couple life together. The only thing that had changed was her curiosity about the arson.

Her phone buzzed in her purse. *Mom.* She hesitated a second and then sent the call to voicemail. The last person she needed to talk to on the day she lost both her job and her boyfriend was her mother, who would tell her to come home and "get back to business" earning a law degree. She just didn't understand that cooking was Bethany's business now.

I'll call her back when I have a new job.

She pushed open the glass doors and stepped out into the refreshing spring afternoon. She paused for a moment, leaned up against the smooth gray marble that clad the outside of the building, and let the brisk breeze wash over her. The tension in her shoulders melted away and she was finally able to sort out her thoughts about her argument with Todd.

Something seemed...off. Breakup aside, why had he tried to hide that he was on Hosanna Street if he had nothing to do with the house fire? Especially since helping George was the perfect alibi—George would have seen him come and go. It just didn't make sense.

Could Todd have been lying about the whole thing? What if he didn't help George at all, and the gasoline was on his shoes because he had used it to set the fire?

But if Todd was the arsonist, why did he choose Amara's house? Why not one of the other historic homes on the street. After all, Amara had been helping the developers, not working against them. It didn't add up that Todd would choose *her* house to destroy, especially not with her asleep inside! He might be callous, but he wasn't evil—was he?

I better talk to George again and confirm Todd's story about the gasoline on his shoes. His version of events will prove one way or another whether Todd was involved.

She shook her head, desperate to clear the cobwebs of suspicion from her mind. *What am I thinking?!* Todd was a capitalist, not an arsonist. He probably broke up with her because he was tired of the smell of french fries, not because he committed a crime.

Her phone buzzed in her purse.

Mom again? Crap, it's Kimmy. The produce had been delivered to Café Sabine. There was no more time to relax in the sun and think about the arson right now—she had a gala to cater.

Chapter 12

"**I** put some stock on the back burner for you," Kimmy said without turning her head. She focused intently on the cutting board in front of her as she minced herbs and chopped onions. "And half this veg is for you. What took you so long?"

"Thanks for the head start. I got stuck at Todd's office." Bethany looped a Café Sabine apron around her neck and washed her hands at the deep copper sink. She nodded hello to Amara, who was breading veal cutlets on the center island, and found a place to set up her work station.

It was always a pleasure to cook in the kitchen here. Light streamed through high, arched windows and glinted from the handmade tiles that lined the walls from floor to ceiling. It was a far cry from the plastic countertops and fluorescent lighting at the Seafood Grotto. Maybe her next job would be somewhere more like this, somewhere with character and class. "I hope I didn't set you back for dinner service."

"Don't worry about it. Auntie helped me, so I'm right on schedule."

"Kimberly made sure you had time for all your hanky-panky." Amara stepped gracefully around Bethany to rinse her hands in the sink, her nose in the air.

Bethany grit her teeth so she wouldn't say something she'd regret. "Actually, it took so long because he broke up with me."

Kimmy gasped. Her knife clattered onto the cutting board as she turned around to face Bethany. "He didn't!"

"I warned you those party pants wouldn't keep a man," Amara said, as she dried her hands on a linen towel. "I know these things."

"Guess you were right." Bethany smiled thinly.

Kimmy shot Amara a warning look. "Auntie, be nice. Does this mean you aren't catering tonight?"

"That's why the conversation took forever. He was afraid to break up with me because he thought I might bail on the gala. I finally told him that I'd cook for it no matter what, and then he ended things."

"What?! You should totally bail! He can't treat you like that and still expect you to cook your heart out for his stupid party." Kimmy crossed her arms and leaned back against the counter.

Bethany sighed. "It's tempting, but I really need the gig. I maybe sort of got fired this morning." She mumbled the last few words to the checkered tile floor.

Kimmy jolted upright, flung her arms around Bethany, and squeezed. "Oh, honey." Bethany felt tears prick the corners of her eyes, but she took a deep breath and shook off the self-pity. There was no time for that.

Amara clucked her tongue. "You girls better get cooking, then. This affair won't cater itself."

"Right again," Bethany muttered. *Why does she always have to be right?!*

Kimmy turned back to her cutting board, and Bethany took a cart and headed for the walk-in cooler, where she retrieved a box of corn on the cob, tiny plump tomatoes and zucchini for the veggie skewers, and lemons and cucumbers to put in the refreshing drink she'd planned. As an afterthought, she grabbed a bunch of basil and another of mint.

She tasked Amara with peeling and slicing the cucumbers and lemons for the water while she made the vegetable skewers. The kitchen settled into the comfortable rhythm of slice and chop until Kimmy broke the quiet.

"Did Todd give you a reason for the breakup?" She brought a bowl of onions, carrots, and celery over to where Bethany was slicing zucchini. "Here's your mirepoix for the corn chowder."

Bethany glanced at the bowl. "That's too much!"

"Didn't I tell you? You're making some soup for me, too. I'm calling it corn *velouté* and serving it with chive oil instead of basil oil. I think everyone in Newbridge is going to have this soup tonight." Kimmy grinned. "That's your payment for giving me relationship deets. Since I don't have a love life, I have to live vicariously through yours."

Bethany shrugged. "He said that if I suspected him of arson, we shouldn't be together."

"Wait, what? You accused your boyfriend of arson?"

"Sort of. Not really. I just asked him where he was that night. Before, he said he hadn't been on Hosanna Street, but then he admitted that he went to Amara's house—to your house," she finished lamely.

"That's right," Amara said, as she slid cucumber slices from her cutting board into a pile. "That boy came to my house on Sunday evening."

Kimmy looked confused. "Why was he there on a weekend? I thought he was more of a nine-to-five guy."

"He said he was inviting her to attend the city council meeting the next day," Bethany explained. "Nothing nefarious."

"I told him to buzz off." Amara smacked the bowl down on the counter. "I said I wouldn't be caught dead at his old meeting."

"I thought you supported the development, though. Isn't that why George was so mad at you?" Kimmy asked.

Amara rubbed her chin. "I did, it's true. At first, I thought they really wanted to make our neighborhood a better place. Seemed like they were helping people out, like they did with my new porch. But then they started expecting things out of me, and I realized it wasn't *help*, it was a bribe. No way was I going to speak up to the city council for them, not even for that cute little boy with the khaki pants."

"He said you agreed to it. Or he let me believe you did, anyway..." Bethany trailed off, trying to remember Todd's exact words. "Maybe he didn't understand what you meant?"

"I gave him a big ol' *no*." Amara snorted derisively. "He begged me to write a letter instead. Said he would even get down on his knees and ruin his khakis if I would say nice things about the development and what it'd do for Hosanna Street. But Sharky knew he was full of something. Chased him clear off the porch."

Bethany giggled in spite of herself as she pictured Todd being taken down by dog the size of a turnip. But Kimmy clearly didn't find it so funny. Her brow furrowed and she bit her lip.

"I think we should call the cop who gave me the business card. You know the one I mean?"

"Officer Perez, right? Charley. Why?" Bethany's stomach knotted. Even though Todd had lied through his teeth about everything, she still had a hard time believing he'd light someone's house on fire.

"She should know about this. We told her about George and the weirdo historical society lady, but we didn't say anything about Todd because we didn't know he had a motive. But you heard Auntie—he was there at her house that night, and he was probably angry and humiliated after he got chased off!"

Bethany nodded thoughtfully. "Plus afraid that he wasn't going to get what he wanted at the city council meeting the next day without Amara's support."

"You call that police woman, Kimmy." Amara shook her finger, her voice quavering. "If you don't, I don't know what I'll do when I see him again. Dirty, low-life user—"

Fear pierced Bethany's chest. What if Amara attacked Todd at the gala? *My career as a caterer will be over before it even gets started.*

She had to find a way to defuse the situation. In her most soothing voice, she said, "We don't know if he had anything to do with it. He said the house wasn't on fire when he left."

"He might have come back later," Kimmy said darkly. She wiped her hands dry on her apron, pulled her phone out of her pocket, and then stopped with her finger on the screen. "Shoot, I left the card at home."

"I have one in my purse." Bethany motioned for Kimmy to follow and led her out to the hall where she'd hung her purse on a hook. She quickly found the cop's card and handed it to her. "Before you call, you should know that she asked me about you. Or rather, about *us*."

"What do you mean?"

"She wanted to know if we were a couple." Bethany waggled her eyebrows and grinned. "I think she might be into you."

Kimmy rolled her eyes. "She was probably just investigating the arson. Newsflash: not all female cops are lesbians, Bethany."

"Not all white dudes who want to build developments in historic black neighborhoods are evil, either, but here we are." Bethany twisted her mouth wryly. "Call Charley."

Chapter 13

Wednesday

"Let me get this straight," Charley said, her pen poised over her notebook. "Now that this guy dumped you, you're reporting him as a suspect?"

"I'm not reporting Todd because he dumped me; we broke up because I—" Bethany began, but Amara interrupted her.

"*That boy* was at my house that night. He wanted me to do this and that for him, and I told him fat chance." Amara shook the white tablecloth out over the food service table like she was cracking a whip.

"Because I caught him lying about it," Bethany finished. She glanced at the clock on the bell tower of the old Hosanna Street church. Guests would be arriving in less than thirty minutes, and they still had so much to do. Hastily, she assembled the burners that would keep the food warm.

"I see. Can anyone corroborate any of this?"

Amara banged a handful of cutlery down on the table. "I corroborate it! My dog Sharky chased him off the dang porch!"

Charley bit her lip, and Bethany could tell she was trying not to laugh. "Ma'am, unless your dog can come down to the station and give a statement, I'd prefer to talk to a human being."

"Todd said he helped a neighbor with his lawnmower after he spoke to Amara. George Washington. He'll probably be here tonight—you can interview him then!" Bethany hefted the huge pot of corn chowder from the cart onto the warmer.

"I remember that guy. He's a real character. Coop and I are working the gala, so we'll be sure to keep an eye out for him." Charley tucked the notebook in her chest pocket. "Appreciate your help. If you have anything else to report, don't hesitate. Tell Ms. Caldwell the same."

"I'm right here!" Amara snapped over her shoulder as she tended to the skewers on the grill.

"Right. I meant your niece, ma'am." Charley grinned at Bethany. "I'll have a chat with this Todd guy, too."

Amara clanged the lid of the grill shut and pointed her finger at the cop. "You better get to that boy before I do. He may not be able to speak after I'm done with him."

Bethany cringed internally. "She doesn't mean that."

"Oh, yes I do!" Amara's face was cold and queenly. "He'll rue the day he set foot on my porch."

Any amusement remaining in Charley's expression faded as she leaned across the food service table toward them. "Listen to me. Do not make a fuss or get in the way tonight. We're fairly certain the arsonist will be at the gala, and she may flee if she gets wind of our investigation. Just play it cool, serve some food, and leave the detective work to us."

"She?" Bethany asked. "You think the arsonist is a woman?"

A smile quirked the corner of Charley's mouth. "No, I don't. Arsonists are usually male. I just try to keep it equal opportunity until I know for sure."

Over Charley's shoulder, Bethany spied the mayor and two city council members entering the church courtyard. "I don't mean to rush you off, but we're about to have some customers!"

Charley looked behind her. "Party's starting. Have a good evening, ladies. If you see anything suspicious, let me know."

Bethany nodded and slid the trays of ice and opened clams onto the long table and stepped back to survey the scene. The creamy corn chowder was hot and a towering stack of espresso mugs teetered beside the pot, ready to be filled. She placed the bottle of fragrant basil oil next to the warmer so it would easy to dot on the top of each tiny serving.

"Skewers almost done?"

Amara nodded and picked up her tongs, swiftly moving the colorful vegetable skewers from the grill to some large silver platters. "They're as perfect as a baby's laugh."

The clams were gorgeous and fresh—Bethany would have to call and thank Jim in the morning. That just left—

"The cucumber-lemon water!" She snapped her fingers and dashed back to the car with the cart. As she returned, lugging the cart behind her, she saw Todd approaching the food service table. He had changed for the party and now wore a crisp, seersucker suit with blue and white stripes.

"Hey!" he called to her. "Looks great! I'm headed to ring the church bell to get this party started, but I just wanted to check and makes sure—"

At the sound of Todd's voice, Amara whirled around, sending an entire try of grilled vegetables flying into his face and across the entire food service table. Bethany stopped short, dismayed. Pieces of zucchini and tomato were strewn across the clams and dotted the surface of the corn chowder. There was no way she could serve any of it!

"Look at my suit," Todd moaned, holding his shirt away from his body. "It's ruined!"

Amara slammed down the now-empty tray. "Ruined? You want to talk about ruined? My house is ruined, that's what's ruined! You burned it to the ground!"

"What am I going to do?" Todd mumbled, still staring at his clothes. Then his eyes lit on the table, and his voice went up an octave. "We can't serve this mess! The mayor is here!"

Bethany rushed over and grabbed a napkin to dab his lapel. "Don't worry, we'll figure something out. We can order pizza!"

"Pizza? We can't serve pizza to the mayor!" Todd pushed her hands away.

"OK, no pizza. Um...how about a taco truck?" She kneeled to pick up pieces of grilled squash off the ground in front of the table. "I have an extra tablecloth to replace this one. It will be fine, Todd, I swear."

"This is not a taco truck event," he yelled, his face turning as red as the tomatoes that stained his shirtfront. "This is a gala—and you're destroying it!"

"Like you're destroying our neighborhood," Amara said loudly, motioning to the small crowd that had gathered. "You tricked all of us just so you could make a quick buck!"

The people around them gasped, and Todd froze. Bethany realized that she was the only one who could defuse the situation. Amara was too angry, and Todd was clearly too anxious about what people thought of him to recover gracefully. She murmured in his ear, "Why don't you head to the bathroom and clean up? I'll take care of the mess out here. Ring the church bell once you're ready to mingle with guests."

He nodded gratefully and walked as quickly as he could toward the church. Bethany turned to the stunned crowd. They were beginning to murmur, wondering what had happened, and that meant rumors were about to swirl. She decided to do the only thing she knew how—cook.

"Well! Thank you for coming! You're just in time for the demo." She stepped behind the table and smiled widely. She motioned to Amara. "My assistant grilled some beautiful tomatoes and zucchini, and we have cherrystone clams straight out of Black Bear Bay. I'm going to show you how to assemble a delicious summer chowder!"

The crowd clapped politely. Bethany noticed Charley and Coop standing in the back of the group, along with the mayor and Don Hefferman. She recognized a few other people too, including Alex Vadecki. He glowered at her, and she quickly averted her gaze. "I have a pot of chowder base here beside me. Shh, don't tell anyone—it's mostly just chicken stock and cream! I slipped a few diced potatoes and some corn in there, and some sautéed mirepoix. Doesn't have to be fancy, folks!"

"What's 'meer-pwah'?" a lady in front asked. "I don't think we have that here."

"Just a little onion, carrots, and celery," Bethany explained. "I'm going to chop up the rest of these grilled veggies and pop them in the soup. They're going to add some color and some smoky flavor."

Thank goodness I brought my knife kit. That kit had seen her through the ups and downs of culinary school, and she still didn't feel right if it was more than an arm's length away.

She gestured to Amara to bring the tray of skewers over, and began deftly sliding the vegetables from the sticks. "Of course, you can roast these in the oven, too, if you're not in the mood to fire up the grill. Keeps the boyfriend busy for a while, though. Or girlfriend—we're equal opportunity around here," she added.

A polite chuckle rippled through the crowd, and Bethany saw Charley give her at thumb's up from the back row.

Maybe not all female cops are lesbians, Kimmy, but that one sure is. Equal opportunity until you know for sure, right? Bethany smiled to herself and scooped the pile of chopped veggies into the pot.

"Now for the star of the show—these little babies!" She gestured to the clams. "Now, you can throw these on the grill and they'll open right up for you, but here's a trade secret: those guys down at the fish market will shuck them, too. Don't bother doing it yourself."

"Aren't you going to cook them?" the same lady from the front row asked.

"These clams are pretty small, so they'll cook in the hot broth. But if you grill them, they'll be fully cooked by the time they open." Bethany felt a surge of satisfaction as she slipped the clams one-by-one from their shells into the soup and tossed their empty shells into a tub under the table. It was more than a little ironic that she had to reconstruct her deconstructed chowder, but she had to admit that the soup looked pretty amazing.

"While the chowder simmers for a few minutes, let me enchant you with my genie in a bottle, also known as basil-infused olive oil!" She grabbed the bottle of bright-green oil and presented it to the crowd with a flourish. The crowd, which grew larger by the minute as more guests arrived, *oohed* and *aahed* appreciatively. "It will in fact grant your every wish—if your wish is to make an impressive summer soup."

Several people chuckled at the joke, and Bethany could tell that most of them had already forgotten the scene between Amara and Todd. A huge weight lifted from her shoulders. This chowder might not snag her a restaurant investor, but it would feed the crowd and maybe, just maybe, lead to another catering gig.

Bells pealed out from the church tower, ringing loudly to announce that the gala had begun. Everyone stopped to listen to their chime. When the sound died away, Bethany smiled widely.

"If you'd like a taste, just form a line right here. You'll see that servers are passing glasses of champagne; please take one while you wait to help celebrate a new chapter for Hosanna Street!"

The people in the crowd chatted eagerly as they migrated into a semblance of a line at the food service table. Bethany took a deep breath, let it out, and took her place behind the table next to Amara.

"Can you dot the basil oil after I serve? Two or three drops per little cup, then put the cup on the tray. Hopefully we can keep up with demand!"

Amara nodded and they settled into the rhythm of service, although Bethany tried to keep her head up to greet each guest as they took a cup of soup from the tray.

The woman who had asked so many questions during the demo smiled a little too brightly when she reached the front of the line. Her red lipstick perfectly matched her sharply tailored skirt suit. She held her hand out across the table for Bethany to shake. "Robin Ricketts, *Newbridge Community Observer*."

Bethany shrugged apologetically and nodded at her gloved hands as she ladled chowder as fast as she could. "Nice to meet you. You're a reporter?"

"I cover crime, mostly. I was hoping to have a word with Ms. Caldwell about her house fire." She extended her hand to Amara, who put down the bottle of basil oil and shook it dubiously. "Robin Ricketts."

"I heard you before." Amara frowned. "Are you the one who wrote the article on Tuesday that said I *claimed* my life was in danger?"

Bethany looked anxiously at the line piling up behind the reporter. "Can this wait?"

Robin glared at her and swiped two cups of soup from the tray. "Fine. I'll come back later."

"Great." Bethany smiled at her and elbowed Amara so she'd get back to service. Amara quickly caught up with the few cups that were waiting for her, and the line once again moved smoothly.

"Wonderful, just wonderful!" Don Hefferman stepped out of line to stand beside Bethany as she pulled ladle after ladle of soup from the pot. "I saw the whole demo. Really impressive the way you handled the crowd."

Bethany felt a rush of pride. "Thanks, Don! I hope it tastes just as good."

He patted her on the back, and she cringed a little. *Too friendly. He must not know that Todd and I broke up.*

"I'm sure it's great," he said. "A little bit *rustic* for me, though. Probably not what I'm looking for as an investment, but good job—great job. Love your attitude. Don't work too hard, now. Make sure you get a glass of that bubbly before it's gone!"

Nothing like someone telling you that they like your attitude to ruin your attitude. No time for this fool. Bethany focused on her ladling and ignored Don until he drifted away.

As soon as Don left, Alex Vadecki loomed beside her. "What do you think you're doing?!"

She didn't turn to look at him, but she could see his purple-red complexion out of the corner of her eye. "I'm catering the party, Alex, like I told you I would."

"That demo was such an attention grab. Are you trying to snipe Hefferman to invest in your amateur hour?"

Bethany glanced worriedly at the line. Were people paying attention to Alex's blustering? She didn't want anyone to get the impression that she wasn't a professional. But they all seemed more interested in the soup than in their conversation, and she relaxed a little.

"For your information, Don passed on my concept. How'd your meeting with him go?"

Alex's shoulders slumped and he ran his hand through his hair. "He's still interested. I mean, he delayed again—for the fourth time—but he said if I develop more training programs for franchisees, he'll be ready to sign on the dotted line."

"Are you sure about that?"

"What do you mean? Is that some kind of dig at the Grotto?" Alex looked ready to explode again.

The short fuse on this guy! Bethany rolled her eyes. "No, it's more of a dig at Don. I heard that he's stretched pretty thin. I'm not sure he even *has* money to invest in a restaurant. All his money is tied up in this condo development project. He didn't expect it to pass muster with the city council, so he overcommitted, and now he has to pay the piper."

Alex purpled again. "Who'd you hear that from?!"

"Todd. Ask him yourself. Last time I saw him, he was headed inside the church."

Alex stormed off, and Bethany heaved a sigh of relief. The guy was like an angry mountain troll, and that couldn't be good for business. She looked up into the lens of an enormous antique camera.

"Smile!"

Bethany obeyed and the flash nearly blinded her. Fancy Peters popped out from under the camera drape, and Amara nearly snarled.

"Just documenting the event," Fancy said coolly. "I'm trying to take photographs of all the people celebrating, so future generations know who to blame." She picked up a cup of chowder, holding out her pinky delicately like she was taking tea with the queen.

"Get out of my face, Ms. Fancy Pantsy," Amara warned.

Bethany gaped for a second and then realized the line was backing up again. "Can you move your gear to the side, please? Just so others can be served."

Fancy scooted the tripod away from Amara, who looked ready to smash the camera, and pointed it at a low brick wall behind the service table. She put her cup down on the table near Bethany and ducked back under the drape.

"Do you take pictures of everything?" Bethany asked.

"I'm documenting the property for posterity. Every detail, if I can. This is all going to be gone when they take a wrecking ball to this beautiful building." Fancy's voice was muffled by the drape.

Bethany looked around. The church was simply built, with a plain brick exterior, straight bell tower, and rectangular courtyard. *Pretty in its own way, but it's no cathedral.* "It doesn't have much architectural detail. What is there to document?"

Fancy screeched and jerked her head out from under the black cloth. "This is the most important church in Newbridge! It's not the oldest or the most ornate, but it's the only one established by freed slaves before the Civil War. It deserves to be remembered, even if it doesn't have gargoyles and stained glass."

"We agree on that," Amara said. "But that's all. This church replaced the one that was built originally. There's nothing special about the bricks, just about the people who placed them. And that boy Todd promised me to put up a monument in the courtyard of the new building. Just because we aren't living in the past doesn't mean we can't remember it."

Fancy glared at her. "Your neighborhood is going to crumble once this church is gone, and you have no one to blame but yourself. Someday this town will regret this night. You'll remember the sound of that church bell ringing for the last time."

As if on cue, bells began chiming again, and Fancy Peters glanced around, bewildered. Bethany looked at the bell tower, equally confused, until she saw Amara pull out her cell phone. The bells ceased as soon as she answered the call. *Ringtone.* Bethany giggled, but Fancy didn't even crack a smile.

"Disgusting invention," she said. She picked up her camera and tripod and left. Bethany looked over at Amara to share a laugh, but Amara held up a finger, the phone still pressed to her ear.

"I have to take this. Won't be a few minutes," she mouthed.

Bethany nodded and motioned for her to step away from the service table. "Don't worry, I got this."

They'd served almost all of the initial crowd of people. Some of the guests in line now were back for seconds, but Bethany recognized some new faces, too, like Amara's neighbor George.

He looked over his shoulder as he approached. "She gone?"

"Who?" Bethany asked.

"Amara, that's who. Is she still thinking I had something to do with that fire? The police keep coming to my house to talk. I already told them everything!"

"Have some soup, Mr. Washington. Good for what ails you," Bethany said. She dotted some of the basil oil onto a cup of chowder and handed it to him.

He slugged down the tiny cup, and his face brightened. Bethany didn't have the heart to tell him that a cop was probably looking for him right now. He moved out of the line to stand by her elbow and surveyed the line passing by the food service table.

"I can't believe all of these folks having a blast now that the development is a done deal." He shook his head and helped himself to a cup of lemon-cucumber water. "They should be protesting! Or maybe something more drastic."

Bethany grinned at him. "For a protestor, you sure seem to like the refreshments. Did you protest when Todd helped you put your mower in the shed?"

His brow furrowed. "How'd you know about that?"

"Todd told me he gave you a hand. I wasn't sure if he was lying about it, but I guess he was telling the truth." Bethany kept her eyes on the line, nodding and smiling as gala guests complimented the chowder. "Thank you. Napkins are on the end, sir. Go ahead and help yourself."

"Even snakes do us a favor sometimes," George mumbled. "Whether that helps or hurts us, who knows."

The pot was getting low, and her wrists were sore from ladling and squeezing the bottle of basil oil. She hoped everyone had gotten their firsts since so many people were back for seconds. It seemed like the whole gala was on an endless loop past the food service table. George was planted beside her though, with no apparent intention of leaving, so she decided to probe him a little more. "Did you see anything else weird that evening around Amara's place?"

He snorted. "Nothing but the usual. Giant swan heads, white dudes with clipboards, crazy lady on a tricycle."

"Wait, Fancy Peters was there on Sunday night, too?" Bethany paused. Maybe Kimmy and Amara were right to think that Fancy had something to do with it. *Maybe Fancy and George were in it together—they certainly had the same opinion of Amara!*

George nodded. "Yup. She's there every day, taking pictures for our permanent record. The good and the bad, she's got it on film."

"Do you know her very well?" Bethany asked innocently. She straightened a few of the cups on the tray and slowed her ladling pace so the soup wouldn't get cold before people drank it.

George shifted where he sat on the low brick wall. "Nah. You just see people every day, and you recognize them. She's no friend of mine."

Bethany noticed they were about to run out of napkins. *Time to grab another pack from the car.* "Where has Amara gotten to?" she wondered aloud.

At that, George stood and motioned to the building behind them. "I'm gonna take a tour of the old church before Amara comes back and bites my head off."

She laughed, but stopped short when she saw Alex heading for her table again, his fists clenched as tight as his jaw. "Uh oh, looks like I'm the one who's going to get their head bit off. See you around, Mr. Washington."

"Where's Todd?" Alex demanded. "Where's he hiding?"

Bethany shrugged. "I don't know! I'm just the help, remember?"

"Don't lie to me. I know he's your boyfriend." Alex glared at her. "The kid has skipped out on his own party. Where'd he go?"

Bethany stood on tiptoe to scan the far corners of the courtyard. Todd was nowhere to be seen. "I haven't seen him since you yelled at him," she said, flustered.

"Since *I* yelled at him?" Alex looked confused. "I haven't yelled at the guy yet."

"Not you—Amara." Bethany turned, expecting Amara to be beside her, but then remembered she had taken a phone call. "Never mind, she's not back yet. He had an argument with Amara that turned into kind of a food fight. His suit got dirty—maybe he decided to go change."

Alex snorted and put both his hands on the table so he could lean toward her. "Your boyfriend's a loser. Don was looking for him, too—said this whole deal might be off if Todd doesn't show his face. You can bet your sweet bippy that I'm going to clinch my franchise deal when the condo development falls apart just like this mess of a party!"

"He's not my boyfriend," Bethany said weakly as he loomed in front of her "I don't know what to tell you."

"Is this guy bothering you?" Charley leaned around Alex and made eye contact with Bethany. A concerned-looking Coop tapped Alex on the shoulder.

"He was just looking for Todd." Bethany smoothed her apron, feeling instant relief. *Thank goodness for Charley!*

"What a coincidence, so were we," Coop said. He nodded to Alex, and Alex swiftly left the table without even a backward glance at Bethany.

"Like I said to him, I don't know. I haven't seen him since my cooking demo. He rang the church bell right after I finished, though. He must be tied up with guests somewhere. The mayor, maybe?"

Coop shook his head. "We've made the rounds—nobody's seen that yahoo anywhere."

"He may have gone home. His clothes were pretty stained after Amara slung the veggies at him. I'm sure he'll be back, though. While you're waiting for him, would you like some soup? I'm about to run out."

Charley peered skeptically over the rim of the chowder pot. "I don't know—what's in it?"

Bethany grinned. "The usual suspects."

"C'mon, Perez! Don't be scared!" Coop jostled Charley's arm.

"Fine. I'll try it. But I can't promise to finish if it has funky things floating in there."

Bethany filled a cup and dotted it with basil oil, then handed it gingerly across the table. Charley took a tentative sip, and her eyes opened wide.

"Wow, this is fantastic! No weird stuff at all. It'd be great if it was a little more spicy, though."

Bethany nodded. "If you solve this case, I'd be happy to make you a spicy version."

Coop rubbed his hands together. "My turn! Don't be stingy."

"Why don't I give you a bowl instead of a cup, then?" Bethany grinned and used the ladle to scoop the bottom of the pot. As she pulled up the ladle, she froze.

There was a gun.

In the soup.

Chapter 14

Wednesday

Coop stared at Bethany. "Is this a joke?"

Bethany stared back. She couldn't tell if Coop was serious or playing some kind of game. *Did he slip that in there when I wasn't looking?*

"I don't know. *Is* it?"

"What's going on?" Charley asked. Bethany raised the ladle higher so that Charley could see the tiny, pearl-handled pistol half-submerged in the creamy broth. "What's that doing in there?"

Bethany shrugged helplessly. "I have no idea. It's not there for flavor, that's for sure."

Coop pulled a plastic bag from a pouch on his utility belt and shook it open. "Can you put it in here? Without the soup, if possible. And try not to jog the trigger while you do it—we don't know if that thing is loaded."

Bethany stretched to reach the grill tongs and used them to fish the gun out of the chowder. She dropped it into Coop's outstretched bag. He sealed it and turned to Charley.

"This gala suddenly got a whole lot more interesting," he said.

Charley nodded solemnly. "If you didn't put that gun in the soup, who did?"

"Is it even real? Maybe it's part of someone's costume." As soon as she said it, Bethany realized how stupid she sounded. Nobody at the party was in costume, unless you counted Fancy's Victorian getup.

"It's real." Coop held the plastic bag up to get a better look at the gun. "It's a classic pocket pistol. You can hide these things just about anywhere—although I've never seen one in a pot of soup."

"Glad you've retained your sense of humor," Charley said dryly. "We don't even know if there's a crime here, though."

Bethany stared into the depths of the pot, hoping it might provide an answer. "Maybe it fell in by accident?"

"Sure, or maybe someone wanted to hide it. We'll try to find the owner and go from there. Who had access to your soup?" Charley pulled out her notepad.

"I mean, I did," Bethany stammered, racking her brain for information. "Um..."

"Amara," Charley prompted. "She helped serve, didn't she?"

Bethany nodded. "Kimmy helped cook, too, but it's not hers."

Coop held his hand up. "Let us draw the conclusions, please. Is she here?"

"No, she's working at Café Sabine. That's where we prepped all the food. But I guess just about anyone here at the gala could have slipped it into the pot."

Coop stretched across the table and pantomimed dropping something into the pot. "I think you'd notice that, don't you?"

Bethany nodded. "Probably. So you think it's either Kimmy's or Amara's? Where is Amara, anyway?" She scanned the gala. George Washington was leaning against a tree, chatting with one of the city council members. She spied the mayor chatting in a small group with Alex and Robin Ricketts, the reporter. Fancy Peters was taking photographs of the church door. *No sign of Amara's turban.* "If the gun belongs to anyone, it belongs to her."

As she spoke the words, Bethany felt a chill run up her spine. *Why would Amara bring a gun to the gala, anyway? Who was she afraid of—or who should be afraid of her?*

Charley moved around the end of the table and stood next to Bethany. "Wouldn't be too hard to slip something into the pot from here without being noticed."

Bethany shook her head. "Nobody came back behind the table. Wait—a few people came over to chat, and I told them to stand here so they wouldn't hold up the line."

"Who was that?" Charley asked.

"Um, I guess Don Hefferman, George Washington"—she ticked off each name on her fingers—"Fancy Peters. Alex Vadecki. I think that's it."

"Good." Charley nodded to Bethany. "If you remember any more, let me or Coop know. I'd like to interview everyone on this list before they leave the party."

"We should let Todd know," Bethany said. She raised her voice. "Anyone seen Todd?"

Every face in the courtyard turned toward her.

"Great," Charley muttered. "Real subtle."

Coop smiled and raised a hand. "Hi, folks. We just have a couple questions."

A buzz ran through the gala. Robin Ricketts stepped forward. She had a small voice recorder in her hand that she held out toward Coop.

"Excuse me, officer, is that a *gun* in that bag?"

The crowd buzzed even more loudly, and most people took a step back from the food service table. A few on the fringe began edging for the street.

"It's perfectly safe, ma'am," Coop said. "Everything is under control. We're just hoping to chat with a few people, starting with Todd."

"Is that *his* gun?" Robin stepped closer to him.

"We didn't say that." Charley tried to herd Robin back into the group of people. "Please, carry on with the party. If we need to talk to you, we will."

"Help!" a voice cried. It sounded far away, but it was perfectly clear. "Call an ambulance!"

The crowd looked up, and Bethany realized the voice was coming from the top of the bell tower.

The voice came again. "Someone's been shot!"

Panic rippled through the gala guests. Bethany felt the blood drain from her face. *Could the gun in my soup have shot someone at the party?* Her stomach roiled at the thought.

"Out of the way, please!" Coop yelled as he ran for the bell tower. The crowd parted wordlessly to let him through.

Charley waved to get the crowd's attention. "Everybody stay calm. I'll call this in." As she gave information over the radio, the mayor stepped out to calm the partygoers. A few people sat down, apparently faint from the excitement. Once Charley finished her call, she, too, ran for the tower.

"I have water over here," Bethany called. She filled cups and put them out on the table, and George Washington came over and ferried water to those who needed it. In a few short minutes, the ambulance arrived, lights flashing. Two paramedics in orange uniforms jumped out of the back and jogged into the courtyard.

"Where's the victim?" the lead paramedic, a tiny blonde woman, asked. Everyone in the courtyard pointed to the bell tower.

The other paramedic groaned as they headed for the door at the base of the tower, a stretcher held between them. "Ugh, stairs."

"Do you know who got shot?"

Bethany jumped. She turned and was surprised to see the reporter at her elbow.

Robin smiled, but the smile didn't reach her eyes. "Didn't mean to scare you. I just thought you might have information. You found the murder weapon, right?"

"Murder? Who said anything about murder?" Bethany looked anxiously at the church doors. "I'm sure the shooting was just an accident."

"You seem to know a lot about it." Robin raised her eyebrows, prompting Bethany to go on.

"What? No, I don't know what's going on. I'm just the caterer, and I only got the job because Todd's my boyfriend—ex-boyfriend," Bethany explained. "I know as much as you do."

"Where'd you find the gun?"

"I was just serving soup to Charley and Coop, and there it was. In the pot." Bethany cringed, remembering the look on Coop's face. "I'm so embarrassed. I can't believe this happened. Who's going to want to eat my food now that a murder weapon was found in it?"

"I thought you said it was an accident?" Robin moved her hand closer, and Bethany realized she was being recorded.

"You said murder, not me!" she stammered. "I didn't say that."

"But you just did." Robin wrinkled her nose, her fake smile still plastered on her face. "You said the murder weapon was in your food. Do you think the murderer put it there on purpose to frame you?"

Bethany's mouth dropped open, but before she could say anything more, the paramedics burst through the church doors with the stretcher. Someone was strapped to it, but Bethany couldn't make out who it was. Charley and Coop were just behind them and helped the paramedics load the stretcher into the ambulance.

Robin sprinted for the ambulance without even pausing to acknowledge Bethany. *Talk about a nose for news. Even though she's dressed up, she wore flats for a reason. Smart woman.*

Just as Robin reached the ambulance, Charley stepped in front of her, preventing her from seeing inside. Robin stamped her foot and tried to push past, but Charley held her off until the ambulance doors closed and the vehicle pulled out of the church parking lot.

The gala started to break up, guests leaving in twos and threes on foot and in cars. Coop tried desperately to keep people in the courtyard, to no avail.

For the first time since she'd pulled the gun up out of the soup, Bethany looked down at the food service table. It was trashed. The soup pot was basically empty, but drips and drops of chowder studded the white tablecloth. The water coolers had been emptied, too, and the trash cans beside the table overflowed with napkins. Piles of dirty champagne flutes and espresso cups were collected in dishpans by the hired servers to be delivered back to the rental company.

Time to clean up my stuff, too. She began loading the cart with items to go back to Café Sabine. *What could be keeping Amara?*

"Bethany."

She looked up and saw Charley standing in front of the table. "What is it?"

"Can someone else clean this up? We need to talk."

"No," Bethany said distractedly, as she stacked the silver trays. "I don't know where Amara is. I'm sure she'll be back soon, though."

"I'll help you, then." Charley grabbed one side of the table-cloth and Bethany grabbed the other. As they folded it, Charley seemed to be trying to transmit something with her eyes.

"Don't you have police work to do?"

"I'm doing it," Charley said grimly. She put her hands on top of the items in the cart to keep them balanced as Bethany pushed the cart toward the car. When they were out of earshot of any partygoers, she sighed deeply. "I'm really sorry, Bethany. I don't know how to tell you this."

"Oh no," Bethany said, her heart going cold. "Not Amara. It can't be. Please tell me she's not hurt."

"It was Todd, Bethany. In the tower."

Bethany skidded to a halt just feet from Kimmy's blue Honda. "Todd shot Amara? Why?!"

"Listen to me." Charley grabbed her by the shoulders and looked straight into her eyes. "Todd has been shot. Todd is the victim."

Chapter 15

Wednesday

"I just can't believe this," Kimmy said, pacing up and down the length of their small living room holding a tattered piece of paper in her hand. She sat down on the couch beside Bethany and put her arm around her, and then abruptly stood up and began pacing again.

"I know." Bethany brushed the tears from her cheeks, but they were immediately replaced with new ones. "I didn't even get to say goodbye to him. I should have gone with him to help him with his suit instead of doing that stupid cooking demo to save face!"

"No, honey." Kimmy plopped down again and gave her a squeeze. "You did what you thought was right. I'm not even that surprised—Todd had a lot of enemies on Hosanna Street. I just can't believe *this*." She shook the piece of paper before handing it to Bethany.

Bethany smoothed out the paper and tried to decipher the spidery cursive handwriting on it. She held it up to the light to make out the words, but half of the note was soggy and shredded. "Sharky is sure living up to his name, isn't he?"

Kimmy glared at the little dog, who cowered under the coffee table. Then she relented and scooped him up, laughing as he began gnawing on her watchband. "He can't help it. He's full of beans, as Auntie would say."

"Well, near as I can make out, this note says 'Take good care of Sharky. I'm going to—' and then the rest is chewed up.

113

You don't think she had anything to do with Todd being shot, do you?"

Kimmy made a skeptical face. "No, it's probably a coincidence. I'll text her and see what's going on." She pulled out her phone and thumbed a quick message. A few seconds later, they heard a *ping* from the kitchen counter. Kimmy groaned. "Of *course*, she left her phone here."

"Is that a coincidence, too?"

Kimmy bit her lip and didn't answer. Sharky whined and pawed at her arm. She put it back down where he could reach it, and he resumed chewing on the leather part of her watch.

Bethany rubbed her forehead. This all seemed so surreal, like she was in a waking dream. Her ex-boyfriend was murdered, the murder weapon was found in her soup pot, and now her newest roommate was the prime suspect. *When had Amara sneaked away from the food table to do the deed? During the demo?*

Her thoughts were interrupted by a loud banging on the door. Sharky yammered his tiny reply, and Kimmy ran to answer the door with Sharky tucked under her arm, still barking. She returned, looking resigned, with Charley and Coop. She motioned to them and sat back down on the couch. "Cops."

Bethany tried to smile in greeting, but the most she could manage was quirking one side of her mouth. "Hey."

Coop shifted uncomfortably as he scanned the room. "Mind if we sit?"

"Suit yourself," Kimmy said. Bethany nodded, and Coop took the armchair.

"I'll stand." Charley shifted uncomfortably. "We came to give you our condolences. We're very sorry for your loss."

"Thanks." Bethany had a hard time even looking at Charley's sympathetic expression. She was afraid if she did, she might start crying all over again.

"We just need to review a few things," Coop said. "Were you at the food service table all evening? No bathroom trips, no breaks?"

Bethany shook her head. "No, none. I unloaded, did the demo, served, then loaded up and came back here."

"And you, Ms. Caldwell? Where were you?"

Kimmy jutted out her chin. "I was working all night at Café Sabine. I had nothing to do with the event."

"But you helped prepare the food for the gala, didn't you?" Coop leaned forward in the chair, and Sharky growled a warning at him.

Kimmy stroked Sharky's head, but it did little to soothe the savage beast, who pulled back his lips to show Coop his teeth. "I did a little to help Bethany prep, but I had my own food to worry about."

"Do you own a gun, Ms. Caldwell?"

"No!" Kimmy put down Sharky and stood up. Coop eyed the dog warily as she strode into the kitchen and began filling the kettle. "Can I get anyone some coffee or anything?"

"No, thank you. Is Amara here?" Charley asked. "We'd like to talk to her, too."

Bethany shook her head. "She went somewhere. It must have been related to the phone call she got. It seemed pretty urgent."

Coop and Charley shared a meaningful look. Coop cleared his throat. "Ms. Caldwell, does your aunt own a gun?"

Kimmy dropped the kettle with a crash and then fumbled in the sink trying to right it. "No! I mean, I don't think so. I've never seen her with a gun. She isn't that type of person."

"The type of person who carries a weapon for self-defense, you mean?" Coop asked.

"The type of person who want to hurt other people." Kimmy put the kettle on the stove and turned on the burner. "She doesn't hold grudges."

"Witnesses at the gala say that she was pretty upset with Todd." Charley flipped through her notebook, scanning several pages. "They report that she threw food and screamed at him. Seems like she might have a grudge there."

"Sit down," Kimmy snapped as she returned to the living room. "You're making me nervous, hovering around like that." Bethany winced and hoped the cops wouldn't take offense, but Charley didn't say a word an took a seat opposite Coop.

"She thought Todd might have had something to do with the arson," Bethany explained. "But she didn't throw food at him. That was an accident."

Charley glanced over her notes. "So she disliked him, had a fight with him, and then disappeared after he got shot. Not to mention that the murder weapon was found where she'd been working all evening. It kind of paints a picture of someone who's guilty."

"She wouldn't hurt a fly," Kimmy said stubbornly, as she sat down beside Bethany and picked up Sharky again, cradling him like a baby. "Look, she left a note telling us where she was going. Why would she do that if she was trying to evade the law?"

Coop cocked his head to one side. "This is the first we've heard of a note. Can we see it?"

Kimmy pushed it across the coffee table toward him, and he picked it up gingerly by the corner.

"Are you kidding me?" he said. "Look at this, Perez. 'The dog ate my alibi.'"

"If we knew where she was, we'd tell you," Bethany said earnestly. "We're worried about her, too. She left her phone here."

Charley nodded. "Let us know if you hear anything from her. Obviously, we have a few more people to talk to, but we want to make sure she's safe. My instinct is that the arson was due to Amara's support of the development project. Her life could still be in danger."

It was ironic that the fire was the reason the whole project was approved, if the arsonist was against the development. But someone who had accidentally helped the condo development move forward might then decide to stop it—by killing Todd.

"You should check George's shed," Bethany blurted out.

"Why?" Kimmy asked.

"Todd said he helped George put his lawnmower in the shed that night. If he has a mower in there, he probably has gas and other stuff in there, too—what accelerant was used in the arson?"

Charley shook her head. "We can't tell you that. Anyway, we don't know; it's still being analyzed."

"Well, check the stuff in George's shed to see if it's a match."

Kimmy frowned. "I don't think George has that much ill will toward my aunt. He's a good guy underneath that gruff exterior."

*A good guy who said more drastic measures might be neces-
sary to stop the development—and who sent Amara a very threatening note.* Bethany didn't want to hurt her best friend's feelings, so she kept her suspicions to herself. "I didn't say George
did it. But whoever did it might have used an accelerant from
his shed. Todd's shoes smelled like gas when I saw him on Monday."

Coop and Charley shared another look.

"What?" Kimmy asked.

Coop shook his head. "Nothing. Just let us know if you
hear anything from Amara." He and Charley stood up from
their chairs.

After the two cops had left, Kimmy made cups of
chamomile tea and sat with Bethany on the sofa as they sipped.
Sharky lay between them, wedged between the two cushions,
and they took turns petting him. He whined and wagged his
tail whenever they stopped.

"Poor little guy. He misses Auntie."

Bethany chewed her lip. "Do you think she maybe was
involved in Todd's murder? I've been going over the evening
again and again, trying to remember when she was there and
when she wasn't. I can't remember whether or not she was there
during the cooking demo."

Kimmy sighed and scratched Sharky between the ears. "We
don't even know *when* Todd was killed, so there's no point in
obsessing over it. I know she didn't do it. I'm sure she'll call tomorrow and tell us the whole story: where she is, why she left
so suddenly, and when she'll be back."

"But what if she doesn't?"

"It doesn't prove anything. All we can do is get some rest and see what happens tomorrow." Kimmy stood and picked up Sharky. "You're sleeping with me tonight, mister."

"Is that the first time you've said that?" Bethany attempted a grin.

"For your information," Kimmy said, sticking her nose in the air, "*yes*. But Sharky is a very special man."

"He is. Night-night, you two." Bethany smiled, but a lump rose in her throat, and she swallowed hard. Todd had been a special man in his own way, and she'd miss him, despite his flaws.

Despite Kimmy's instructions to get some rest, Bethany tossed and turned, unable to shut off her brain. She couldn't make sense of what had happened. She'd somehow lost her job and her relationship on the same day that Todd lost his life, and now Kimmy's aunt was missing. Was there one explanation for all of these things? Or was it all just a terrible coincidence? Kimmy thought Amara might have the answers, but Bethany had her doubts.

Why would Amara run away and leave her phone behind? *She has more to hide than anyone else.*

Chapter 16

Her phone buzzed at 6:30 a.m.

Bethany was already awake and making french toast for breakfast, but she didn't answer. A few minutes later, it buzzed again, and Bethany sent the call straight to voicemail.

Kimmy fed Sharky and poured them both some coffee, then sat down at the table. "Who are you avoiding?"

"Mom." Bethany slid plates of piping hot, cinnamon-y goodness onto the table and drizzled syrup over the top of each. "She doesn't need to know that I lost my minimum-wage job—at least not until I get a new one. Plus, she loved Todd, and I do *not* want to have that conversation right now."

"Totally understandable," Kimmy said. She stood up and headed for the front door. "Hang on, I think the newspaper just hit the porch."

Bethany put the french toast pan in the sink and ran water in it, then slid into her seat at the table just as Kimmy returned with the paper. "Any headlines about the gala?"

"Oh no," Kimmy said, her eyes fixed on the front page. "Oh *no*."

Bethany tried to grab it out of her hand, but Kimmy jerked it away. "You don't want to see this!"

"Well, now I do!" Bethany got up and circled behind Kimmy's chair to look over her shoulder. She was horrified to see a huge, unflattering picture of herself on the front page. Her mouth was open, and she was clearly in a heated discussion with someone, but that person was cropped out of the photo.

120

"When was this even taken? The newspaper reporter didn't have a camera."

Kimmy shrugged. "It was definitely at the gala last night."

Bethany snapped her finger. "I bet it was Fancy Peters. She had a huge old antique camera that she said was to document the event. She probably took this when I was talking to Alex—he accused me of trying to steal Don's investment out from under him."

"Jerk," Kimmy said. She folded up the newspaper and put it under her napkin. "You don't need to read that."

Bethany pretended she was headed back to her seat, but at the last minute nabbed the paper from under Kimmy's napkin. Kimmy squawked in protest, but Bethany shushed her. "I need to know what's being said about me. Plus, I have to look at the classifieds—mama needs a new job, remember?"

She unfolded the paper and scanned the article.

· · · ·

CRIME CHOWDER

By Robin Ricketts

Newbridge, CT—Residents of Hosanna Street were shocked last night when prominent developer Todd Luna was shot and killed at a gala celebrating his newest project.

The murder weapon, a Browning pistol, was found in a pot of clam chowder that was served to gala guests by the victim's girlfriend and event caterer, Bethany Bradstreet.

As Luna's body was loaded into the ambulance, Bradstreet expressed concern for her reputation.

"Who's going to want to eat my food now that a murder weapon was found in it?" she asked this reporter.

Is Bethany Bradstreet a black widow spider who has devoured her mate? Or is she merely a ruthless businesswoman looking to profit after a tragedy? Whichever web she weaves, she's full of spin.

Officers investigating the case are interested in the whereabouts of Amara Caldwell, Bradstreet's catering assistant, who may have information related to the crime. Residents with any related knowledge should contact the Newbridge Police.

· · · ·

BETHANY'S HANDS SHOOK and her breakfast threatened to make a reappearance. "It's worse than I thought."

"I'm not going to say 'I told you so,' but..." Kimmy sighed sympathetically.

"It's all lies!" Bethany blurted out.

"I know. You didn't say that stuff. It's just sensationalist journalism."

Bethany stared out the window at the fishing boats in the marina. "Well, I did say that, but I didn't know that the body was Todd at the time! She makes it sound like I didn't care about him at all. Plus, it says I'm his girlfriend, and we were already exes!"

"Not sure that detail would improve the story, though," Kimmy said dryly. "The breakup might strengthen your motive to off Todd. Don't worry about it too much. The cops know you didn't do it. You're not in any trouble."

Bethany let out a deep breath and tried to ease the tension in her shoulders. "You're right—you're right. I need to shake it off."

Her phone buzzed again. *Mom.* Bethany realized with horror that her mom had probably gotten the newspaper, too. She groaned and sent the call to voicemail. "That's why she's calling so early! She saw the story."

"At least the article doesn't say you lost your job?"

Bethany made a face. "That's not exactly the silver lining I was looking for."

Kimmy took the paper back and paged through until she got to the classifieds. "I'm going to find you some great jobs—better than the Grotto. You're going to get a new gig, you're going to get a new man, and we're all going to live happily ever after."

Bethany nodded. She could tell Kimmy was worried, too, but she was thankful for her friend's brave face. They couldn't both fall apart at the same time. Kimmy perused the help-wanted ads while Bethany finished her coffee. By the time she reached the bottom of the mug, Kimmy had circled three ads in red pen. She pushed them across the table.

"That's a start, anyway. You should stop by those places today—it'll keep your mind off the whole Todd thing. And by the time you get back, Auntie will have called to set things straight with the cops."

Bethany scanned the ads. The circled jobs were all at places on the same trendy street downtown. It'd be easy to visit them on her bike. "Thanks, Kimmy. I owe you one."

Kimmy pushed back her chair and cleared their dishes to the sink. "You can buy me a root beer float when you get one of those jobs."

"Deal." Bethany smiled, enjoying the first surge of hope she'd felt in more than twenty-four hours.

Chapter 17

Thursday

The manager of Hole Foods peered at Bethany's resume. "Says you have fryer experience."

Bethany nodded, twisting her hands nervously. "I've been working the fry station for about six months at my current job—I mean, my last job."

"Any desserts?"

"Seafood, mostly. But I'm sure I can fry a doughnut—frying isn't rocket science."

The manager looked at her doubtfully over his thick-framed glasses. "We'll see about that. Why don't you fry up a couple and then glaze and decorate them. You can use any of our doughs or toppings—I want to see some creativity!"

"You got it!" She rolled up her sleeves and got to work. *Never thought I'd be thankful to Alex for putting me on the fry station.*

First, she fried a chocolate éclair and a vanilla doughnut to puffy perfection. She filled the éclair with salted caramel cream and topped it with chocolate ganache and edible rose petals. She chose a simple orange glaze and candied-ginger sprinkles for the doughnut and presented both to the manager while they were still warm.

He took a bite of each, savoring them like fine wine. "Hm. Not bad. Your fry is spot-on, and we can work on the flavors. How do you feel about early mornings? We start frying at four a.m."

"Early mornings are fine. I'm up with the birds."

"Great! Let me give"—he checked her resume again—"Mr. Vadecki a call over at the Grotto. If he has good things to say about you, you can start on Monday!"

Bethany's stomach clenched at the mention of Alex, but she nodded. "Great. I'll see you then." She held her head high as she pushed her way out of the doughnut shop, but she wanted to crumple on the spot.

No way Alex will give me a good recommendation. He said he would make sure I never work in Newbridge again!

Hopefully, the next restaurant wouldn't be a stickler for checking references. She slipped the page from the newspaper out of her purse and checked the next address. Only a couple blocks up—she didn't even need to unlock her bike. It was a hipster restaurant called Toast with the Most. She spotted it easily; the front door of the restaurant was shaped like a giant piece of bread.

Bethany scanned the menu posted in the window. Toast, toast, and more toast. Toast with jam, toast with cinnamon-sugar, and of course, toast with avocado.

And I thought frying was boring—toasting isn't even cooking! But a job was a job, so she pushed through the bread-door and walked straight up to the counter.

"Can I talk to the manager? I'd like to apply for the Toast Engineer position."

The woman behind the counter had blonde hair in two braids, and freckles dotted her nose. The wooden nametag pinned to her apron said her name was Clementine. "Um, we don't really believe in managers at Toast with the Most. We're kind of a collective, so nobody is in charge, you know?"

Bethany did not know. She was used to a typical restaurant kitchen, with a dictatorial head chef and a bunch of underlings doing his or her bidding. She had no idea how a restaurant without a leader could possibly work. *Guess I'm about to find out.*

"OK, so who does the hiring? Can I talk to that person?"

Clementine smiled patiently. "We all have to agree."

"I have to interview with everyone who works here?" Bethany blinked, glancing around the restaurant in an attempt to count employees. "How many is that?"

"Let's see." Clementine looked up as she counted mentally. "There's Jared, Brianna, Hester, John B., Cheryl, Sunshine, Savannah, John C., Kyler, Larkin, and Gretel. So eleven? Plus me. Twelve. You'd be lucky number thirteen in our toast family." She beamed at Bethany.

Bethany sighed. *Nothing like a twelve-person interview panel for a gig making toast.* She stuck out her hand. "Let's do this thing. I'm Bethany Bradstreet. It's nice to meet you."

Instead of shaking Bethany's hand, Clementine stepped back, looking horrified. "You're not the one, are you? The one from the newspaper who killed her boyfriend?"

"I didn't kill him!" Bethany said quickly, looking over her shoulder to see if any of the restaurant patrons had overheard.

"The article said you did. It said you hid the gun in your soup, too!" Clementine shuddered and reached for the phone. "I don't think we can have someone like that working here. We respect our ingredients."

Bethany almost burst out laughing. "You think I'm going to hide a murder weapon in the avocado or something?"

"We do work with *knives*." Clementine waved the phone at Bethany. "I'm sorry, but I'll have to call the police if you don't leave. We really can't have you hanging around here and taking hostages or something."

Bethany held up her hands. "I just need a job. I'm not trying to bother anyone." She backed slowly out of the restaurant, keeping her hands in the air. When she pushed through the giant piece of bread onto the street, she dropped her hands by her sides, defeated.

Two down, one to go. Maybe the third time's the charm? She pulled the newspaper page out of her purse to check the last advertisement Kimmy had circled.

"Pickle packer at the Big Dill?! That's not even a cooking job!" The words flew out of her mouth before she could stop them, and she looked around hurriedly to see if anyone was paying attention. Thankfully, no one was passing by on the street, but Bethany noticed Clementine staring suspiciously out the window at her.

Talking to myself on the street corner is definitely not helping my cause. She pulled out her phone so she could pretend she was making a call. She dialed her voicemail box and held the phone to her ear.

"How can I find a job in this town if my references sabotage me and my face is on the front page as the prime suspect in a murder investigation? Charley and Coop know I had nothing to do with it, but how can I get everyone else to believe that, if the only thing they know about me is what they read in the newspaper?" She stopped short and hung up her fake call.

Of course.

If the only person people listened to in this town was Robin Ricketts, then that's who she needed to talk to.

Chapter 18

Thursday

The offices of the *Newbridge Community Observer* were shabbier than Bethany expected, housed in a crumbling storefront behind the warehouses at the marina. She double-locked her bike to a light pole and cautiously made her way to the dark glass door.

Inside, fluorescent lights lit worn carpet. The reception desk was empty except for a telephone and a sign that said "Please Call Your Party's Extension." Bethany ran down the short list until she found "Crime" and dialed the two-digit number.

"Crime desk."

"Hi. I'm in the lobby. I need to speak with Robin Ricketts about the murder of Todd Luna. Is she in?"

The voice laughed. "Honey, I'm the whole department. Come on back. Third one on the left."

Bethany headed down the hallway as instructed. The door to the third office on the left was open, and she could hear strains of country-pop filtering out. When she stuck her head in, Robin motioned for her to enter.

"Bethany Bradstreet! What a nice surprise. I take it you saw my piece. Front page!" She patted a purple chair and then sat in another one behind the orange melamine desk. A huge aquarium burbled behind her, filled with darting fish in neon colors. "Sit, sit."

Bethany sat. "I wouldn't call it a nice surprise. The article is kind of a problem for me, actually."

Robin opened her eyes very wide and tilted her head to the side, batting her eyelashes innocently. "How so?" Her hand snaked across the desk and turned on her voice recorder.

Bethany eyed it warily and chose her words with care. "Some of the...*inaccuracies* in it have made it difficult for me to get a job, for example."

"Inaccuracies? Like what?" Robin pushed a copy of the paper across the desk toward her.

Bethany scanned the article, trying not to look at the terrible photograph of herself while she did so. "Well, for example, Todd and I actually broke up. He wasn't my boyfriend when I catered the gala."

"An ex takes revenge," Robin murmured, scribbling notes on her desk blotter.

Bethany smacked the desktop with her hand. "See? That's exactly the kind of thing I'm talking about! I didn't take any kind of revenge. And that awful quote you printed!"

"Angry ex takes revenge." Robin scribbled out something and scrawled another line on the blotter.

"I wasn't angry at him." Bethany crossed her arms.

"Coldblooded ex takes revenge?"

Bethany wanted to scream with frustration until she saw the twinkle in Robin's eye. "You're not serious."

"No. Obviously not. I talked to the cops, and they said you had nothing to do with it."

"Then why spin it like I was involved? Why print that nasty quote? I didn't even know it was Todd when I said that!"

"You're the one who said it." Robin shrugged. "It seemed pretty callous no matter who was strapped to that stretcher."

"And it got you the front page," Bethany said bitterly.

"That, too. And hopefully the front page story will shake a few witnesses loose. We all want that, don't we? Isn't that why you're here—to help solve Todd Luna's murder?"

"Turning the whole town of Newbridge against me isn't very helpful in that respect."

"So what do you want from me?" Robin asked, leaning back in her chair.

"I'm here for a retraction!"

"Not going to happen. Everything in that article is true."

Bethany snorted. "Truth is in the eye of the beholder, then. I don't see how that article is going to lead anyone closer to finding the real murderer! Todd had a million enemies in town, but I wasn't one of them."

Robin leaned forward, tapping her manicured fingernails on the desk thoughtfully. "Tell you what. You tell me what you know, and I'll do my best to point suspicions in the right direction. Maybe we can break open this case together."

Bethany hesitated, unsure whether she could trust Robin. *The best route to clearing my name—and Amara's—is to find the real murderer, though.* Bethany nodded, and Robin opened her laptop.

"Let's start with those enemies you mentioned. Who disliked Todd so much? He seemed like an upstanding member of the community, invested in improving rundown neighborhoods."

"He was," Bethany said. "Sort of. But he's also very interested in making money. A lot of the people on Hosanna Street weren't big fans of the development, but he didn't really take their feelings into consideration. He bribed homeowners to go along with it, too."

Robin, who had been typing at Bethany talked, paused. "Bribed? What do you mean?"

"He gave money to people with historic homes—for improvements or additions. That was partly so they'd have goodwill toward the development, and partly so they'd make updates that might knock them off the historic register so the city council would approve the project. That didn't make him any friends at the historical society, either."

"I see." Robin made a few more notes on her computer. "How do you know this? Do you have proof?"

Bethany shook her head. "He just told me. But his secretary, Shirley, might have some paperwork to back it up."

"Do you think you can get it from her?"

Bethany thought back to the last time she'd seen Shirley. She'd definitely heard their contentious breakup through the office door. "Doubtful. She wasn't a big fan of me, and the last time I saw her, Todd and I had just fallen out."

"Well, I think the historical society probably has a copy, too," Robin said. "Maybe we can get it from them."

"What? Why would the historical society have a copy of Todd's files?"

"Not his files—the sale agreement. They already had paperwork drawn up." Robin must have noticed the confusion on Bethany's face. "The historical society was planning to buy the church from Todd if the development deal wasn't approved by the city council. You didn't know?"

"No!"

Robin nodded. "It was kind of a big deal. They were fundraising like crazy to come up with the money to buy it."

"So they had even more reason to block the deal. No wonder Fancy Peters was so crabby at the gala. She's an odd character. Todd said she was always hanging around Hosanna Street, taking pictures and harassing his people."

Robin waved her hand. "Fancy's harmless. She takes so many photos because she uses them for her souvenir stand. I'm pretty sure she runs the historical society for the sole purpose of getting monuments put up around town. Then she takes pictures of them and sells the postcards at her kiosk in the train station."

"Doesn't that give her a strong motive to kill Todd? She's probably pretty happy now that the condo development won't happen."

"Maybe. Although maybe she would have made more off her photos of the church if it had been demolished. And who knows what will happen with the church now that Todd's dead. His investor might follow through with the project. Just because the development is derailed doesn't mean it won't happen eventually. Hm, 'Derailed Development.' Could be part of a good headline." Robin tapped a few keys.

"So, question," Bethany said. She reached over and clicked off the voice recorder. "If you don't think Fancy is involved, and you don't think I'm involved, who's your prime suspect?"

Robin closed her laptop and leaned her elbows on it. "Isn't it obvious from my article?"

"I thought you were pointing the finger at me!"

Robin shook her head. "Nope. Read it again."

Bethany picked up the paper and skimmed the article again. When she got to the last line, she gasped. "Amara! You said to call the police if they knew where Amara was, because she might have information about *me*."

"I didn't say that. I said she might have information about the murder. Everything in that article is true."

"Almost everything," Bethany reminded her. "Anyway, you lead the reader to *believe* that I'm the main suspect, and Amara might know something about what I did."

"That's right. Nobody will turn her in if they think she might have done it. But they will if they think it will help catch another person who did."

Very clever, Ms. Reporter. Bethany realized she'd underestimated Robin Ricketts, and she debated for a minute whether to grab the voice recorder and try to erase it before she left, to avoid having her own words used against her. But Robin seemed to hear her thoughts. She picked up the recorder and tucked it away in her desk drawer.

"You think Amara was trying to stop the development?" Bethany asked.

Robin shook her head. "From what her neighbors say, she didn't really care about the development. I think she was just angry about her home being destroyed."

"And Todd is the one who set the fire."

Robin swiveled her chair and dropped some fish food into the aquarium. The fish crowded to the top of the tank to gorge themselves. "I didn't say that."

"But you must think it."

"I don't think anything. I just report what other people think." Robin swiveled back around to face Bethany and smiled.

"But you said you thought Amara killed Todd!" Bethany protested.

"That's not what I think—that's what the police think. The law enforcement theory is that Todd caused the fire, and Amara killed him as retribution. I have no opinion, although all the facts thus far support that theory. That's why I asked readers to contact the police department, not me." Robin stood. "Thank you for coming in, Ms. Bradstreet. You've been very helpful."

"I have?"

"Oh, yes." Robin held out her hand to shake, and Bethany stood up awkwardly to grab it. "Let me know if you get your hands on any of Todd's paperwork. I'd love to see it. The quicker we can break open this case, the quicker we can repair your image."

"Thanks." Bethany felt dubious that Robin Ricketts had any intention of helping her, but at least she offered a shred of hope that this nightmare would all be over someday. "I'll see myself out."

Bethany left the newspaper office reeling with all the new information. She couldn't believe half of what she'd heard in Robin's office. *Todd was in talks with the historical society to sell the church to them?!*

He'd seemed so confident about the project being approved. Making a "plan B" wasn't like him. He must have really been convinced that the development deal wouldn't be approved—or maybe the sales contract was just a ruse to get the historical society off his back while he got approval another way. *Just another one of his strategies.*

As she unlocked her bike from the light pole, she wondered about Robin Ricketts's strategies, too. Why was she asking

Bethany to poke around Todd's office for paperwork, when clearly she had contacts all over town? And why had she given Bethany so much information—far more information than she'd gleaned?

It must be some kind of test—or a trap. But Bethany wasn't about to step into it without some due diligence. Maybe Robin was lying, feeding her false information so she'd be willing to take a risk she wouldn't otherwise—like sneaking into her murdered ex-boyfriend's office. Before she did anything stupid, she needed to confirm Robin's story. Maybe Todd hadn't made a sale agreement with the historical society at all.

Only one way to find out.

Chapter 19

Thursday

Fancy's souvenir stand was cluttered with photo postcards, figurines, spoons, pamphlets on different historical topics, umbrellas, cast iron pans, old-fashioned lanterns, and t-shirts. There were even shirts for Historic Hosanna Street. The kiosk was so cluttered that Bethany didn't even see Fancy inside until she spoke.

"Why are you here?"

Bethany spotted her behind a rack of maps and smiled in her general direction. "In the train station?"

"No, in my kiosk," Fancy said dourly. She was dressed all in black, like a Victorian widow, complete with a hat and veil. "I don't see a ticket in your hand, and the next train isn't for an hour, so I expect you came to see me."

"You're right," Bethany admitted. "Your comments about the church at the gala sparked my interest in Newbridge history. I thought this would be a good place to start learning more about it."

Fancy's face brightened under her the black netting of her veil. She pulled a map from the rack and held it out. "You're right, this is a good place to start. Open it. All the places of historic significance in Newbridge are marked on it. I have pamphlets and postcards for every one, and you can pick them up individually as they interest you."

Bethany unfolded the map and pretended to study it. "Ah, the church is listed here! I wonder what will happen to it now that Todd Luna is gone."

Fancy pushed back her veil. "The historical society is going to purchase it for land value! We plan to convert it into a museum and cultural center. It'll make Newbridge a destination for history tourists!"

So Robin was telling the truth—the society had *planned to purchase the church.* Bethany smiled politely. "What a wonderful legacy for the town."

"It's lucky the development didn't happen." Fancy smiled back at her and then flipped through a box of photographs sealed in plastic sleeves. She held up a picture of the church bell tower. "Look! I printed some of the film I took at the gala."

Bethany's stomach turned. *Todd was probably laying dead inside the tower when the photo was taken.* "Lucky? Someone died."

Fancy shook her head. "I didn't mean that. I meant lucky we were able to work something out. Don Hefferman has lost enthusiasm for the development now that Todd is no longer spearheading the project. He was happy to honor the sale agreement we'd already drawn up."

I bet he was. He needed his cash back so he could invest it elsewhere—like in Alex's restaurant franchise. Could Don have killed Todd to get out of the investment deal?

"How much for the map?" Bethany asked.

"Seven-fifty. But I'll give you the society discount if you think you might join. So five even."

Bethany dug five bucks from her purse and handed it over.

"Did you want the church photo, too? It's only ten with the discount."

She didn't really want it—in fact, a souvenir of that night was pretty much the last thing she wanted—but Fancy looked so eager that she didn't have the heart to turn her down. She found two more fives and paid Fancy, intending to toss it in the trash on the way out of the train station.

"The society meets on Tuesdays!" Fancy called as Bethany left the kiosk, headed for the trash can by the bakery. "At the library! Hope to see you there."

Bethany nodded and waved, and then stood by the garbage can waiting for Fancy to turn around so she could get rid of the photo—that terrible photo. But just as she was about to shove it in the trash, she noticed a sign taped in the bakery window: Help Wanted.

Well, why not—I'm already here. She tucked the map and the photograph under her arm and pushed through the door. She was hit immediately with a wave of cinnamon. Then luscious vanilla lapped on its heels, and the scent of orange was not far behind. *This wouldn't be such a bad place to spend the day.* Being a pastry chef had never been her goal, but baking wasn't a terrible thing for a chef to add to her resume, either. It was certainly better than pickle packing.

She cleared her throat as she approached the counter, where a silver-haired woman with a pleasant expression on her face was icing cinnamon rolls. "Excuse me, I—"

"Yes dear, one second. I just want to get the last of these finished before they cool off too much. There, now. Done. I'm Olive Underwood. What can I help you with?"

"I just wondered—do you get the newspaper here?"

Olive's face fell. "We used to, but we just canceled our subscription. Things are a little tight. I'm sorry. There's a tea shop up the street that might have a copy."

Bethany's heart soared. Maybe she hadn't heard about what happened at the gala! "That's fine. I saw your help-wanted sign on the window and wondered if I could apply. I'm a trained chef, and I'd love to learn how to bake."

"Would you, now?" Olive's eyes twinkled. "That's wonderful. I'm afraid our position is only a few hours per day, though, and it's just running the register. I could show you a few baking techniques in your off hours, if you wanted. I'll be honest—I'd pictured giving the job to a high school student, not a trained chef. It's just a summer job."

Bethany sighed. "Thanks anyway. I probably need something closer to full-time. Although at this point, I should probably take whatever I can get, so Kimmy doesn't get stuck paying my share of the rent."

"Are you talking about Kimmy Caldwell?"

Bethany nodded. "She's mentioned you before—she works across the street at Café Sabine and sometimes she brings home desserts from here."

Olive clasped her hands together and beamed. "She's a former student of mine! I was a social studies teacher for twenty-five years before I opened the Honor Roll, and Kimmy was a favorite. You two are friends?"

"We met in culinary school, actually. Now we're roommates."

"Well, isn't that lovely? That's certainly a point in your favor if you decide you want the counter job."

"Thanks—I'll keep it in mind." Bethany sighed internally. *Low wages, no cooking, just a few hours—a dream job it was not.* Plus, Olive was likely to find out about Todd and the gala in the next few days, which was sure to change her opinion about who she'd want standing behind the counter at her bakery.

"Here, hon." Olive held a bakery box out toward her. "This is for you girls."

Bethany took it automatically. "What is it?"

"My famous strawberry cream cake. It's Kimmy's favorite, and the strawberries are from just down the road. Picked this morning."

"What do I owe you?" Bethany balanced the box in one hand and reached for her purse with the other.

Olive waved her question away. "Not a penny. Just enjoy."

"Thank you." Bethany got a lump in her throat as she said goodbye and left the bakery. Olive's kindness was touching after a long day of rejection and disappointment. She knew Kimmy would appreciate a bit of sweetness when she got home from work, too—she was likely sick with worry over Amara's sudden disappearance.

Should I tell her that Amara is the prime suspect in the police investigation? Bethany gnawed on her lip as she strapped the cake box to the cargo rack on her bike. If Kimmy knew, she might try to hide her aunt from the police, which would make Amara look even more guilty. But maybe Amara *was* the killer. She had every reason to want him dead if he destroyed her home.

If he destroyed her home. The only evidence the police had that Amara was involved was their belief that Todd had committed the arson. They probably weren't even investigating that crime anymore! She paused, hand on her bike lock. *Maybe I should kill two birds with one stone and see if I can find anything in Todd's office—evidence of either crime.* She might be able to clear Todd's name and her own, if she found the right piece of paper.

She locked the bike up again, unfastened the cake from the rack, and strode confidently toward Todd's office.

Chapter 20

S hirley barely looked up from her desk when Bethany entered the lobby. "How can I help you?" she asked icily.

Bethany proffered the cake box. "I brought this for the office. You know, for all of you, because of Todd—" she broke off and pressed the back of her hand to her mouth, willing her eyes to moisten. It wasn't hard to manage, given the last couple of days' events. "I know how much he loved you all. Like family."

Shirley softened like a cookie in milk. "Now, now. Have a tissue." She took the cake box from Bethany and set it on the desk, swapping it for a Kleenex box. "We're all broken up about it."

Bethany dabbed her eyes with it, carefully gauging Shirley's reaction. She seemed to be buying the grieving girlfriend act—not that Bethany wasn't sad about Todd's death. She was. But a ball of emotions—anger, confusion, fear—surrounded the core of grief, and that made mourning difficult until the murderer was caught.

She blew her nose into the tissue and then raised her head. "Do you think maybe I could peek in Todd's office?"

Shirley frowned, and Bethany was reminded of the time Todd called her a pitbull.

"I just wanted to get the"—she forced a hiccup—"pictures of us together. That's all."

Shirley sighed. "Don't you have copies? Anyway I thought you broke up. I heard you fighting that day. Plus"—she slid a copy of the newspaper across the reception desk toward Bethany—"there's this."

Crap, that stupid article again. Bethany hid her face in the tissue, snuffling noisily, while she thought of a reply. She decided to go with the truth. "I don't know why they printed such horrible things. I didn't even know Todd had been murdered until after he'd already been taken away in the ambulance. I didn't have a chance to say goodbye!"

This time real tears came out and leaked down her face, and she didn't hide them in the Kleenex. "He didn't even have a chance to reimburse me for the catering expenses."

Shirley's frown turned into a sympathetic grimace. "You poor thing. Maybe he left a check for you on his desk. I'll let you in so you can get your pictures and have a look." She looked over her shoulder to see if any of the staff were watching, and then led Bethany down the hall. "I'm the only one with a key," she said.

"He trusted you." Bethany smiled weakly at her, and Shirley looked pleased as she unlocked and opened the door.

"Take your time," she said. "I'll be right out front if you need me."

Bethany slipped inside. Todd's office was exactly as it always was, sleek and tidy. But somehow the modern gray interior seemed sad and spare now, rather than chic as it usually did. *At least it won't be too hard to find things in here.*

She quickly rifled through the files in his desk. There was no catering check in sight, of course. There were blueprints, project plans, and marketing mockups. Nothing too interesting.

She went to the bookshelves, where a photo of the two of them at a gallery opening stared back at her. *Our first date.* Of course that would be the photo Todd would choose, when they were both dressed up and picture-perfect. She picked it up and carried it with her—Shirley would be suspicious if she returned without it. She replaced it with the photo of the bell tower she'd bought from Fancy Peters.

Nothing else on the shelves jumped out at her, so she tucked the photo under her arm and opened the cupboards underneath. These were less tidy, full of outdated brochures and old notebooks. She picked up the one on top and flipped through the first few pages. *Bingo.*

The notebook was full of names and addresses on Hosanna Street, many with little stars by them. Some of the starred addresses also had dollar amounts. Bethany scanned the list for Amara's name and found it—it had both a star and a dollar figure. The amounts of money must indicate what Todd had paid homeowners for property improvements. But what were the stars? Maybe which ones he'd approached?

She noticed George Washington's name below Amara's—his also had a star and a dollar amount. *But he didn't take money from the developers, did he?* George was always solidly against the development in the neighborhood. Did he lie about that to keep his neighbors happy and then secretly work for Todd? Suddenly the story about Todd helping George with this lawnmower made sense, if they were in cahoots.

She ripped the page out of the notebook and shoved it in her purse. *Now what about the sale agreement with the historical society?* She glanced around the room, but there didn't seem to be any other places that Todd could have stored paperwork, unless it was on his computer...or unless it had already been removed and was in someone else's office now.

Like Don Hefferman's.

She stuck her head out the door to see if anyone was in the hallway. All clear. Don's office was just a couple of doors down. She closed the door to Todd's office behind her and walked quickly to the door marked "Hefferman." It was open and no one was inside. She'd have to be quick—Don was likely to return any minute.

Unlike Todd's pristine desk, Don's was a jumble of paperwork, action figures, crumpled snack packages, and dirty coffee cups. Bethany picked delicately through the pile. Underneath a Doritos bag and one of the coffee cups, she spied it—the church sale agreement. She picked it up and flicked through the pages. All signed, sold well below assessed value.

Wow, he really wanted to get that property off his hands. She snapped a photo of each page with her phone. She reached to set the agreement back down where she found it, when she spied another set of official-looking papers underneath. She edged it out from under the pile and almost choked on her tongue when she read the first page.

Alex got his way, after all. The Seafood Grotto had just signed a franchise deal for twenty new restaurants, courtesy of Don Hefferman Investments. The signatures were dated that day; they must have signed the papers this morning. *So that's why Don wanted to unload the church property so quickly.*

She started taking pictures of each page with her phone. Charley would be interested to see evidence that a couple more people had a strong motive to get Todd out of the way. This franchise deal was big money! Before she could capture the last few pages on her phone, she heard footsteps coming down the hall. Hurriedly, she tossed the paperwork back on the desk and scooped trash on top of it.

"What are you doing in here?" Shirley asked sharply, rounding into the office.

Bethany smiled sheepishly and waved the framed photograph to distract Shirley as she tucked her phone back into her purse. "I was so emotional that I got turned around. I was just leaving."

Shirley pursed her lips. "Likely story. I'll see you out to make sure you don't get lost this time." She took Bethany by the elbow and ushered her toward the lobby exit. On the way past the reception desk, Bethany swiped the cake box. Shirley noticed and gaped like a fish, but Bethany just shrugged at her.

"I guess I'm over him," she said and grinned as she pushed through the door.

Chapter 21

Kimmy laughed uproariously. "I can*not* believe you took the cake back!"

Bethany giggled and took another bite of strawberry cream cake. "Aren't you glad I did, though?"

"Definitely. I needed this. Olive was a sweetheart to send it home with you."

Bethany nodded. "I'm seriously thinking about taking the counter job there—although she'll probably change her mind about it once she reads all the scandal and stuff in the paper."

"You don't think Robin Ricketts is going to correct those impressions now that you've gone to talk to her?"

Bethany munched a strawberry and thought about it for a minute. "She said she would. But I'm not sure I trust her completely."

"Then you should think about taking all those pictures from Don's office to the police station tomorrow." Kimmy swiped her finger around her plate and licked the whipped cream she'd collected.

"I don't think they'll be too happy to hear I've been breaking into people's offices." Bethany paused with the last bite of her cake balanced on her fork. "Maybe I will, though, if you come with me and update them on what you heard from Amara. If she didn't do anything wrong, she won't be in trouble."

Kimmy face fell. "She'll be back when she can, but I don't want them to make her come home if she's not ready."

"So you're going to pretend you didn't hear from her?" Bethany wrinkled her nose. Kimmy was usually so principled—it was a little shocking to see her consider hiding something from the police.

"Her sister Pearl is really sick. This could be the last time they'll be able to see each other. I don't want to take that away from her."

"And you don't want her to go to jail."

Kimmy nodded slowly. "That, too."

"I don't want that either."

Kimmy grabbed her arm and looked her in the eyes worriedly. "So you don't think she did it? You're not angry with her?"

"I don't see how she could have."

Kimmy sighed with relief. "I can't tell you how much that means to me. Why are you so sure? Honestly, I started thinking maybe she had something to do with it myself."

"I've been going over the night again and again in my head, trying to figure out her movements. Amara definitely helped me during the demo. She handed me vegetable skewers—I remember that—and she helped me serve soup when it was done. Then the church bells rang to announce the beginning of the gala, so Todd was still alive then. And Amara didn't leave the table until she got the phone call from her sister and left. Nobody saw Todd during the entire night, so he must have been killed right after he rang the bells."

Kimmy gasped. "Maybe that's how the killer knew where he was!"

"We have to tell Charley and Coop about all this stuff tomorrow." Bethany cleared the plates and rinsed them in the sink. "Maybe we should bring them some doughnuts. I made some pretty great ones during my interview at Hole Foods."

Kimmy giggled and pushed back her chair. "That's a little on the nose, don't you think? They might be offended."

"We'll call them beignets, since you're a French chef." Bethany grinned mischievously. "We can mix up the dough tonight."

Kimmy nodded, but she hardly seemed to be paying attention. She got up and peered behind the couch in the living room. "Hey, did you put Sharky out on the patio when you came home?"

Bethany shook her head. "No, I totally forgot about him!"

"Uh oh." Kimmy slowly turned to look at her. "Then where is he?"

A crash echoed from the back of the cottage, and both women dashed toward the noise. "The bathroom!"

When she entered the tiny bathroom, Bethany immediately spotted Sharky cowering in the tub. Normally the shower curtain would have concealed him, but the curtain had been shredded from the floor to about three feet up—as high as Sharky could reach when he stood on the edge of the tub, she imagined.

"Oh holy heck," Kimmy breathed behind her. "How did that tiny little dog do all of this?"

Bethany looked around. Not only was half the shower curtain in tiny pieces all over the floor, but the roll of toilet paper was mangled beyond recognition and all the towels were missing corners. To top things off, both their toothbrushes were on the floor and bore distinct tiny teeth-marks.

Bethany started to giggle, and then she couldn't stop. Sharky wagged his tail hopefully as he stared at the two of them, and that set Kimmy off, too. They laughed and laughed until Bethany's stomach hurt.

Chapter 22

Way too early in the morning, Kimmy and Bethany worked together to shape and fry the beignets while they drank their coffee. In the corner of the kitchen, Sharky gnawed happily on a soup bone Bethany dug out of the freezer for him. She'd been saving it for stock, but in the interest of the rest of their possessions, she figured she'd sacrifice it to the dog.

"One of us has to dog-sit him today," Kimmy declared as she watched him gnaw away at it. "I don't want that to be my shoes next."

Bethany nodded in agreement as she dropped a few more beignets into the pan of hot oil. "If you take him this morning, I'll watch him while you're at work."

Sharky dropped the bone, jumped to his feet, and started barking insistently.

"It's OK, pup, I promise to be nice."

Kimmy rinsed the flour off her hands and dried them. "He's barking at the paper. I just heard it land on the porch." She went to retrieve the paper while Bethany poked at the beignets. They were perfectly golden, and Bethany closed her eyes momentarily, imagining what they were going to be like when they were done—crispy outside, soft and pillowy inside, dusted with powdered sugar. Sweet little clouds that would melt in the mouth.

When she opened her eyes to check on the beignets, she noticed Kimmy casually stuffing the newspaper between the couch cushions.

"What are you doing?" She looked back at the pan in front of her—the beignets had risen to the surface and were ready to come out. She moved them to paper towels to drain and plopped in a few more squares of raw dough. "Another batch done. We're close to being finished."

"Great. I'll just grab a shower, and then we can go. Do you mind frying up the last few without me?"

"Nope." Bethany sprinkled the beignets with powdered sugar and waited until Kimmy had left the room, then grabbed the newspaper from the couch. It was obvious that Kimmy had tried to hide it from her, or at least didn't want to be around when she read whatever was in there.

She unfolded the paper and sat down at the kitchen table.

• • • •

DEVELOPMENT DERAILED

By Robin Ricketts

Newbridge, CT—The much-anticipated 50-unit condo building planned for the site of the old church on the Hosanna Street has been jettisoned. The death of developer Todd Luna at Wednesday night's gala celebrating the project permanently ended plans for the development.

Mayor Strauss expressed regret. "The development would have attracted young tech workers to an aging neighborhood and infused our city with much-needed cash."

Residents of the neighborhood visited the scene of the crime to leave flowers and handwritten cards praising the victim.

"He was a nice kid," said longtime Hosanna Street home-owner George Washington as he placed a bouquet of wildflowers at the base of the bell tower. "He will be missed."

Bethany Bradstreet, ex-girlfriend of the victim, disagreed. "Todd was mostly interested in making money," she said. "He had a million enemies in town."

Police are still investigating the crime.

• • • •

EVEN WORSE THAN I THOUGHT it'd be. So much for a truce with Robin. She'd been stupid to talk to her with that tape recorder running. She pitched the newspaper in the recycling bin.

Kimmy came back looking sheepish. "I tried to keep the water off the floor, but it was tough with only half a shower curtain!" She grinned at Bethany, but her face fell when she saw Bethany's expression. "You read the paper?"

"Yup."

"Still want to take your photos to the reporter?"

"Nope. I think she wants to be the one to drive the murderer out into the open, and she doesn't care who gets hurt along the way. The only thing that will make this go away is solving the case."

Kimmy nodded sympathetically.

Bethany sighed. *I can't count on anyone to salvage my reputation but myself. And the only way to do that is to solve this crime.*

Chapter 23

Bethany and Kimmy stowed two baskets of beignets and one churlish chihuahua into the back of the Honda and drove down to the Newbridge Police Station. It was an old-fashioned building, clad in local limestone and brick, and Bethany felt very nervous as she looked up at it while they unloaded their goodies.

"He only ate two!" Kimmy said triumphantly, as she snapped a leash on Sharky's collar.

Bethany chuckled. "Make sure there's no dog drool on any of the others!" She looped the other basket over her arm and headed for the imposing front doors of the station.

"We're here to see Officer Cooper," Kimmy told the deputy at the front desk, a woman with close-cropped red hair and rosy cheeks.

"Out of the office. He'll be back around two."

Bethany looked at Kimmy, and then back to the deputy. "We have information to report related to the Todd Vega case. And beignets, if you'd like one."

The deputy pushed back her chair and stood up to reach into Bethany's basket. "Well, why didn't you say so?" She spotted Sharky and did a double-take. "Is that a dog or a doughnut?"

"He may have eaten one or two in the car." Kimmy giggled and brushed some powdered sugar off the top of his head. Sharky shook, sending a cloud of sugar flying all around him.

"Glad he saved one for me—this is delicious." The deputy munched on the beignet and motioned for them to follow her down the hall.

"Folks to see you, Charley," she said, knocking on an already-open door. Charley jumped to her feet when she saw them, straightening her uniform. "It's about the Luna case. And they have doughnuts."

"Thanks, Mariah."

The deputy nodded and left.

"Beignets, actually," Kimmy said, holding out her basket. When Charley reached for one, Sharky growled and charged at her feet.

"Hey! Ow!" Charley shook Sharky off and looked down, dismayed. "This little guy is a menace."

Kimmy grimaced. "Sorry. He's very protective. Usually of my aunt, but I guess since she's in New Orleans, he—"

"Amara Caldwell is in New Orleans?" Charley's eyes widened. Sharky made another lunge for her pant leg, and she jumped backward.

"Sorry!" Kimmy said again. "So sorry. I'm really embarrassed." She set the basket on Charley's desk and stepped to the back of the room. She scooped up Sharky and held him firmly under her arm. "Take one now—take two. I'll make sure Sharky behaves."

Charley picked one up, raised it in thanks, shrugged, and took a bite. "Oh, wow. Wow. You made these?"

Bethany nodded. "Kimmy's family recipe. Her aunt grew up in New Orleans and brought the beignet recipe with her when she came to Connecticut."

"To answer your question, that's why she's in New Orleans now—to see her sister, Pearl," Kimmy added quickly. "That's why she left the gala so quickly. Pearl is really sick."

Charley crammed the rest of the beignet in her mouth and grabbed a pencil from the desk. She jotted a few notes in her notepad as she chewed and swallowed. "How do you know this? She contacted you?"

Kimmy nodded. "She called and left a message while I was at work."

"You have the number on caller ID?"

Bethany shook her head. "We don't have caller ID. Costs an extra five bucks, and nobody calls our landline anyway. Not usually."

"I have the address," Kimmy offered. "Great-aunt Pearl doesn't have a phone at home. Auntie probably called from a pay phone. She left her cell at our cottage by accident."

Charley grabbed another beignet and grumbled to herself while she ate it. She finished, licked her fingers, and said, "I have to admit, I'm shocked you came forward with this. It really shows character."

She smiled at Kimmy, and Bethany was surprised to see Kimmy blush as she smiled back. *Aw, cute—Kimmy must have a little crush on Officer Perez.*

"Thanks. I—I just want to help."

"This is very helpful. I'll be in touch with the New Orleans police so they can make the arrest, and then we'll figure out how to transport her back here." Charley grabbed a third beignet.

"The *arrest*?!" Kimmy sank into the chair by the door. She was so surprised that she forgot about holding Sharky, and the dog leaped to the floor and ran toward Charley again, leash dragging behind him. Charley yelped and jumped on top of her desk, throwing the beignet at Sharky in an attempt to slow the dog's attack.

Sharky barked and barked, racing around the desk, while Charley grabbed more beignets from the basket to pelt the dog. Bethany cracked up laughing. Kimmy sat frozen in her chair, still looking horrified, as she watched the scene play out.

"Control your dog!" Charley yelled. "If he bites me, I'll bite back!"

The image of Charley biting a dog-shaped doughnut popped into Bethany's head, and she howled even harder.

Kimmy dove for the end of Sharky's leash and reeled him back in. When she finally got him under control, she had tears in her eyes, and they weren't from laughing.

"Thank you." Charley climbed gingerly down from the desk and began picking beignets up off the floor and depositing them in the trash can. Bethany stooped to help her.

"I just don't understand why you're arresting her," Kimmy said, furiously wiping the tears away with the back of her hand. "You have no proof she did anything wrong—and she's eighty years old!"

Charley sighed. "Everyone at the gala saw her blow up at Todd and accuse him of burning down her house. It's clear she wanted to exact revenge. She may not have intended to kill him, but that was the result. She's the only one with a motive, and she's the only one who fled the scene of the crime. It's obvious she's guilty."

Kimmy started crying harder.

Bethany shook her head. "She's *not* the only one with a motive. A lot of other people benefited from Todd's death—way more than Amara did. All she got was revenge, and we don't even know if Todd is the one who set her house on fire, so maybe not even that!"

Kimmy raised her head. "And she didn't run away to hide—she ran to her sister's house because she was needed there. You know exactly where she is now. Isn't that proof that she wasn't trying to get away with a crime?"

Charley rubbed her forehead, leaving behind a smudge of powdered sugar. "I don't know what to think. What did you mean when you said a lot of people benefited from Todd's death? I can't think of one."

"Don Hefferman, first off." Bethany remembered the uncomfortable conversation she's had with him at the gala. What had he called her soup? Too *rustic*? What a lame excuse. "He was counting on the condo development falling through, so he invested in other projects. The first thing he did after Todd died was sell the church to the historical society. He couldn't get rid of it fast enough!"

Charley raised an eyebrow and scribbled notes as fast as she could. "Go on. Who else?"

"Well, the historical society made out like a bandit. They picked up the property for next to nothing."

Charley paused, pencil on paper. "But the historical society couldn't have known that Don would sell to them, right? After Todd's death, Don could have proceeded with the development using the existing plans."

"I guess so. But they're not the only ones who walked away with a prize, either. Alex Vadecki signed a franchise deal with

Don the morning after Todd died. He basically got the investment money that Don had earmarked for the condo development!"

Charley jotted that down, too. "Do you have proof of any of this?"

Bethany pulled out her phone and showed her the photos she'd taken in Don's office of the documents. Charley's eyes widened as she flipped through them.

She swore quietly under her breath. "I have to show these to Coop when he gets back."

Bethany yelped and swiped for the phone, but Charley was too quick and stepped out of reach.

"You can have it back in a minute. I just need to extract the photos. It'll be faster if you help me out a little." Charley handed her a slip of paper from the desk drawer—a technology release form, with a section to write her lock screen password. "I won't mess with any personal stuff."

"Except my photos, clearly," Bethany grumbled, as she filled out the form and tried to remember if she'd taken any weird selfies lately. *Probably.*

Kimmy cleared her throat. "Does this mean you'll cancel the warrant for my aunt's arrest?"

"I can't promise you anything," Charley said sympathetically. "I wish I could. But we'll at least hold off on having the New Orleans police make the arrest until we investigate these other leads. It's possible that when Amara comes back into town, we'll arrest her then."

"Too bad you didn't spend so much energy investigating the arson," Kimmy said bitterly. "If you'd arrested Todd right away, he'd still be alive."

Charley grabbed the last two beignets from Bethany's basket and went to sit by Kimmy. Sharky flattened his ears and bared his teeth, until Charley tore off a piece of the pastry and offered it to him. Sharky licked it greedily, and then wagged his tail and put both his paws on Charley's leg to beg for another bite.

"I've thought about that a lot," Charley said, stroking Sharky's head gingerly. "I want you to know that I'm still working on the arson case. It could help you down the road to collect the insurance money. Even if Amara goes to jail for the murder, you should be able to collect as her next of kin if the report proves she didn't start the fire."

"How can you prove that, though?" Kimmy asked tearfully. "It seems like you'll never have a definitive answer without a confession from Todd, and he's dead."

Charley munched the other beignet, considering her answer. "Well, we determined that the accelerant used was kerosene. I think Todd probably spotted it in George's shed when he helped him with the lawnmower and used it to start the fire later. It was likely a spur-of-the-moment decision, sparked by his anger at her for refusing to publicly support the development at the city council meeting."

"You found the kerosene in George's shed?" Bethany asked.

"We haven't searched it yet. This is just a rough theory now, based on what you said about Todd smelling like kerosene on Monday, and the tests coming back a match for kerosene."

"I said he smelled like gasoline." Bethany narrowed her eyes, thinking back to the newspaper article she'd read that morning. George was quoted as saying Todd was a *nice guy*—but he'd told Bethany that he thought of Todd as "Stinking Bob," a far cry from a nice guy. George was definitely a liar...but was he a criminal, too?

"What if the arsonist wasn't Todd? What if it was George?"

Kimmy drew in her breath sharply. "George wouldn't hurt a fly!"

Bethany turned to her. "It all makes sense, though. He was angry with Amara about her dog. He wanted to punish her—his threatening note proves that. And he also lied about hating the developers. He was working with them!"

"George? Are you kidding me? All he could talk about what how much he hated the idea of those condos being built."

"That's what he said then, but remember his quote in the newspaper this morning? He said Todd would be missed and that he was a nice guy. He even left flowers at the church for him."

Kimmy frowned. "He was just being polite."

Bethany searched her purse for the piece of paper she'd torn out of Todd's notebook. She held it out to Kimmy. "Look. That's a list of homeowners on Hosanna Street. The starred names are people Todd offered money to for home improvements. The dollar amounts are the ones who accepted the payment. George is on the list!"

Kimmy stared at the paper silently, and then held it out to Charley, who had been flicking through Bethany's photo albums on her phone, emailing them to the department. She handed the phone back to Bethany and then took the paper from Kimmy. Her forehead creased as she read the names and amounts. "Did you make this list?"

"No—I ripped it out of a notebook in Todd's office."

Charley flipped the paper over to look at the back. "It doesn't say that who wrote this. Could have been anyone. And it doesn't say what those stars and amounts mean, either. This is meaningless, I'm sorry to say." She gave the paper back to Bethany, and Bethany felt tears prick her eyes.

"Will you at least *ask* him if he was working with Todd? Because if he was, then he'd have two motives to burn down Amara's house: his own grudge and helping the development move forward."

Charley sighed. "I have to go over there today and search his shed for the kerosene anyway. I suppose I can ask him while I'm there." She looked at Kimmy. "Would you like to come with me? You know him better than anyone, and he might open up more if he's talking to someone from the neighborhood."

Kimmy nodded. "I don't want him getting bullied into saying something he'll regret."

"I'm coming, too!" Bethany said, tucking the list of names back in her purse. "I hope George doesn't mind a visit from Sharky."

Chapter 24

The charred remains of Amara's house cast a grim shadow across the lawn and sidewalk. Kimmy shivered when they got out of the car, even though the midmorning sun was bright and warm.

Bethany put a hand on her arm. "You OK with doing this? You don't have to. I can drive you to work right now and we can forget it and let the police do their job."

A squad car pulled up to the curb next to them, and Charley rolled down the passenger window. "Hey, how'd you get here before us? Were you speeding?"

"No!" Kimmy squeaked. Then she saw Charley's mischievous grin and laughed. "I'm from the neighborhood. I know all the shortcuts."

Coop and Charley got out of the squad car and all four of them walked up the path toward George's front door. Bethany held Sharky's leash and was surprised that he seemed quite content to follow behind them. He didn't even try to bite Coop's ankles.

"You ladies stay behind me," Coop said as he knocked on the door.

Kimmy rolled her eyes. "He's a lot more likely to come at you than at me!"

Coop looked alarmed, but he didn't have time to reply before George jerked open the door. He wore a faded blue bathrobe over his clothes and had on a pair of house slippers.

He looked Coop up and down and shut the door again. Coop turned to Charley.

"Should we call for backup?"

Kimmy didn't wait for Charley to respond. She elbowed Coop out of the way and knocked on the door again. "Mr. Washington? Are you OK?"

George opened the door again, this time only a crack. "That you, little Kimmy?"

"Uh huh. I know you're tired of talking to cops, but they have some questions that maybe you can clear up."

"House is a mess." "

"They just need to see the shed," Bethany blurted out. She leaned so she could see around Coop and Kimmy. "Hi, George."

George opened the door all the way. "All right," he grumbled. "But this is the last time. And keep that dog on his lead."

"Of course." Bethany nodded and leaned down to give Sharky a pat.

George led them all around the side yard to his shed and unlocked the door. He waved them inside. "Whole lotta nothing in there."

"Thanks, Mr. Washington," Charley said, stepping inside. "Do you always keep this shed locked?

"Yup. Gotta keep out the riff-raff." He crossed his arms and leaned against the side of the shed, looking up at the sky like he didn't have a care in the world. "Not that it's working."

Charley and Coop made their way slowly through the shed, checking out the mower and the equipment hanging on the walls. Coop perused the cans and bottles that lined a set of shelves a the back of the shed. Bethany and Kimmy started to enter behind them, but Charley waved them back.

"Don't come in. And don't touch anything!" she said sharply, as Bethany reached for a canister on the workbench.

Bethany jerked her hand back like she'd been burned. "Sorry!"

Abruptly, George started walking briskly back toward the house, surprisingly spry for his advanced age. Kimmy and Bethany looked at each other worriedly.

"What's he doing?" Bethany asked in a low voice.

"I hope he's not making a run for it," Kimmy whispered. "That'll just make him look guilty of something."

Exactly—because maybe he is. But Bethany didn't say anything. She stole a glance at Charley and Coop, who were making a list of all the contents of the shelves. They apparently hadn't noticed that George was gone. She looked back at George's house to see if she could spot him, but its windows were dark and empty.

What could he be doing in there? Is he retrieving a weapon?

"Maybe he just needs to use the restroom," Kimmy said, as if she could read Bethany's thoughts.

"Maybe." Bethany gnawed her lip and glanced back into the shed. Sharky whined at the end of the leash and tugged Bethany toward the lilac bush. "You find anything yet?"

"Just cataloging," Charley said absentmindedly. She looked up from her clip board. "Why?"

"No reason," Kimmy said hurriedly.

Bethany pulled Sharky back toward her. There was no point in upsetting George further by letting the dog pee on his precious plants, especially if he was the kind of guy who'd burn someone's house down.

Coop ducked his head through the doorway and stepped out onto the grass. "No kerosene," he said. Charley lingered in the shed a few moments longer, double-checking their work, but then she came outside, too.

"Where's old George?" she asked Kimmy.

Kimmy nodded toward the house. "He went inside."

"Huh," Coop said. "Should we worry about that?"

"Give him a minute and then we'll go check." Charley looked unsure, though, and Bethany didn't blame her.

Sharky made a running start toward the lilac again, and Bethany hauled him back. "Stop it! Rotten dog."

Kimmy let out her breath in a rush. "See? He's back."

Bethany saw George walking toward them stiffly, carrying a tray of glasses and tiny sandwiches.

Coop chuckled. "Refreshments! Now that's a classy guy. I wish everybody brought us snacks when we searched them."

Charley rolled her eyes. "Good luck with that. Most people don't thank us."

"Most people we search are guilty of something." Coop grabbed a sandwich from the tray and popped it in his mouth. He grinned and, with his mouth still full, said, "PBJ. My favorite."

George set the tray down on the shed's workbench. "I'm not saying there's a nip of moonshine in the lemonade, but I'm not saying there's not, either."

Bethany and Kimmy giggled and each took a glass. Charley and Coop looked at each other, shrugged, and took some, too.

"If we keel over, you're going to the big house," Charley said to George, raising her glass to him.

He winked at her. "Just thought you looked a little parched going through this dusty old shed of mine. Find what you were looking for?"

Charley ignored his question. "You notice anything missing?"

He shook his head. "I keep it locked up. Everything's where it should be."

"Do you have a big problem with theft around here?" Coop looked up and down Hosanna Street, but the sidewalks and street were clear.

George took a long drink from his glass of lemonade. "I wouldn't say people steal. But they borrow and forget to return things now and then. I just like to keep tabs on my items, you know what I mean?"

"Of course." Coop munched another miniature PBJ and licked his fingers clean. "Ever keep kerosene out here? Like for emergency lanterns and stuff?"

George frowned. "Nah. Too dangerous to store that stuff out here where it could build up fumes and explode. Anyway, I prefer battery lanterns that I can keep in the house. I don't want to be fumbling around the shed on a dark winter night looking for kerosene."

Charley nodded. "Sure, makes sense. Sorry to bother you with all this. We just thought the arsonist might have used something from your shed to start the fire. But if you're sure it was locked on Sunday, then—"

"It was—didn't you hear me? I always lock it up. I locked it that night right after that Todd fellow helped me move my mower into the shed. May he rest in peace." George swiped his hand across his face, a gesture of respect or guilt, Bethany couldn't tell.

She couldn't hold back her question any longer. "Why did you take money from the developers? I thought you hated them."

George stared at her, eyes wide. "How'd you know about that?"

Kimmy's mouth opened in disbelief. "So it's true!"

He rubbed the back of his neck sheepishly. "They were giving out free money. Amara got some—why not me, too? Weren't any rules about how to spend it. I told them I was going to build a fence, and I still might." He stuck out his chin, daring them to criticize his decision. "If Amara rebuilds, I'll still need to keep that overgrown squirrel out of my yard."

Sharky yipped and twirled at the end of the leash. Bethany sighed. "I think he needs to go potty," she said. "Is it OK if I let him go in the yard?"

George snorted. "See what I mean? Go ahead. Take him around behind the shed where I don't have to watch."

Bethany led Sharky around the small building while Charley and Coop finished their paperwork. Behind the shed, the yard was less well-kempt, the ground muddy and weeds showing their faces here and there.

"Go on," she said to Sharky, and the dog puttered around looking for a good spot. While she waited for him to finish his business, she dug in the mud with the toe of her shoe, idly uprooting a dandelion that had sprouted there. Then she stopped and looked closer at the ground.

"Charley!" she called sharply. "Come look at this!"

Charley rounded the corner. "What is it?"

Bethany pointed and Charley squinted at the shapes in the mud. "What is it?"

"Those are bicycle tracks," Bethany said. "Not bicycle—tricycle. See how there are three parallel tracks? And look at this." She touched a dip in the ground. "There are three of these, too. Those are the marks from a tripod!"

"I don't follow."

"Fancy Peters! You know, the historical society president? She rides an old-fashioned tricycle, and she takes her big antique camera everywhere. George told me that she was hanging around the neighborhood on Sunday. She might have been here taking pictures on the evening of the fire. Maybe she captured something on film!"

Charley nodded thoughtfully. "That's a really smart idea. Nice work, Bethany. I'd never have thought to look in the mud for clues."

Bethany giggled and patted Sharky. "I can't take the credit—it was all him!"

They walked back out and joined the others by the shed just as George was locking up.

Kimmy glanced at her phone and winced. "I have to get to work. Do you want me to drop you back home, Bethany?"

"No, I don't want you to be late. I'll hitch a ride with Charley and Coop, if they don't mind."

Charley shook her head. "We'll take you, no problem."

Coop looked surprised. "I didn't know we were in the public transportation business. Maybe you had a little bit too much of that lemonade, if you know what I mean."

"Are you really gonna go there?" Charley raised an eye-brow. "Because I kept count on the lemonade, and I'm pretty sure you had three glasses."

Kimmy giggled, and Charley grinned at her.

Coop sighed. "I'm outvoted."

"And I'm driving," Charley said.

Chapter 25

Friday

"Where should we drop you?" Charley opened one of the rear doors of the squad car.

Bethany shrugged. "I literally have nowhere to be. Home is fine."

Coop groaned. "That's across town! Can't you take the bus?"

"Stop being such a grouch." Charley shut the door behind Bethany and went around and got in the driver's seat. When Coop was settled, still sulking, in the passenger seat, she pulled the car away from the curb and said, "Why don't we hit Peters's house on the way to Bethany's? That'll save us a few miles, anyway."

Bethany's ears perked up. "Can I come in with you?" She was dying to see the inside of Fancy's house. If it was anything like her fashion sense, it'd be entertaining to say the least.

"Apparently you can do whatever you want," Coop said, slurring his words slightly. "Because Charley here has a crush on your friend."

Charley whacked him on the arm without taking her eyes off the road. "Go home, Coop, you're drunk."

"So can I?" Bethany asked hopefully.

"Sure." Charley deftly turned the car onto a side street that was only a few blocks long. The little pocket neighborhood of ornate Victorians was well-manicured, and most homes on the street were freshly painted in a rainbow of colors. Charley stopped at one of the most exuberantly painted, a cacophony of aqua, teal, and burgundy, with a bright pink front door. "This is it. Coop, you better stay in the car until you sober up. We don't want you scaring the nice lady."

Bethany followed Charley up the charming front steps to the pink door. Charley knocked lightly, and they only waited a few moments before Fancy answered.

"Yes?" she asked. She wore a white, high-necked blouse with a ribbon tied around the collar, and a long gray skirt with ruffles at the bottom. Her hair was arranged into a softly swooping updo, and she wore tiny round glasses on her nose, as thought they'd just interrupted her reading. Seeing her without her dark veil, Bethany realized that Fancy was much younger than she'd thought—in her late thirties at the oldest.

Charley showed her badge. "I was hoping we could talk to you about the day of the arson. Were you on Hosanna Street last Sunday?"

Fancy frowned. "I can't recall. I'm there often."

"We hoped you might have some photos from that day," Charley pressed. "You're known to often have your camera with you, and the film could provide some evidence."

"George Washington said he saw you that evening," Bethany added politely. "Around the time Todd Luna was there, too. Maybe you remember?"

Fancy's stern expression broke into a smile. "Ah, yes. I was there with my camera. I saw Todd help George with his mower. I think I even got a shot of it."

"Any chance we could see the film?" Charley asked.

Fancy opened the door wide and motioned them inside. "Come in and have a cup of tea while I find the negatives."

Bethany followed Charley down the long wallpapered entry hall to a cozy sitting room. A round table at the center was already set for tea, and Fancy retrieved two more fluted teacups and saucers from the nearby china cabinet. She motioned to the plump upholstered chairs around the table. "Please, sit down."

They sat and she poured them each a cup of black tea. She pushed the sugar and creamer toward them. "Doctor it up while I run to the darkroom."

"You have your own in the garage?" Charley asked.

"Homes of this era didn't include garages," Fancy said. "I outfitted my shed, instead. I develop all the film and print all the photographs that I sell, like the one you bought."

Bethany raised her eyebrows, impressed. "That's really cool. Not many people do that in the age of the digital camera."

Fancy pulled her skirt out and gave a little curtsy. "I'll be right back."

"Wait—while you're out there, can you bring in any from Wednesday night's gala, too?"

Fancy hesitated. "I'll look and see. I don't think I've developed the film from the gala yet."

"Yes, you have!" Bethany said. "I bought a picture of the church tower from that night, remember?"

"Oh, that's right." Fancy smiled. "I'll see what else I have out there."

"Bring what you have," Charley said cheerily as Fancy left the room.

Bethany stood and looked out the window. She wanted to make sure Fancy had left the house before she spoke. She saw Fancy exit through a side door and head across the lawn toward a small windowless shed, painted in the same colors as the house. "Why do you think she said she hadn't developed the film yet?" she asked Charley. "She had a whole stack of photographs of the old church from the gala when I visited her yesterday. Plus she took the photo of me that was in the paper on Thursday morning. She must have the developed the photos on Wednesday night after the gala!"

"Maybe she just forgot." Charley sipped her tea.

If the cop's not suspicious, then maybe I shouldn't be, either.

Bethany watched Fancy look over her shoulder before retrieving something from underneath a small garden statue. *The key to the shed?* Sure enough, Fancy used the item to unlock the darkroom door and then slipped inside.

"Better drink some of this tea before she gets back," Charley said. "If George hadn't just fed us sandwiches, I'd be scarfing down these scones. Look at them! I'm going to take one back to the car for Coop."

Bethany came back to the table and admired the pastries and sipped tea until Fancy returned with a stack of black and white photographs.

"Here you are," she said, and handed the stack to Charley. "Some from Sunday, some from the gala." She poured herself a cup of tea and nibbled on a crisp lemon cookie, never taking her eyes off of Charley.

Charley spread the photos out in front of her, separating the ones from the gala into a neat stack.

"There's Todd's beemer!" Bethany said, and pointed to a photo that clearly showed the front end of Todd's prize possession parked along Hosanna Street. "He was definitely there on Sunday. And look, there's a picture of the same angle and you can see George's shed. Todd's car is gone, and the shed is locked up, just like George said."

"The arsonist brought the accelerant," Charley murmured, staring at the photographs. She scooped the Hosanna Street photos to the side and spread out the gala photos in their place.

"Give me all the photos of the food service table," Bethany said. She picked a few out of the pile and Charley handed her a few more. Bethany set them out in neat rows in front of her. "This one is from the beginning, when we were setting up! See? Amara is at the grill working on the vegetables still."

She put that photo at the top left. She picked up another photo and squinted at it. "Do you see that? I think it's Todd's arm near the water cooler. His suit was seersucker—pretty distinctive. I think this was right before he and Amara argued." She passed the photo to Charley.

Charley stared at it dubiously. "I can't tell who it is. When I saw Todd, his suit was covered in food—so I can't say whether or not that's him."

Fancy cleared her throat and reached out with a delicate, pale hand. "Mind if I take a look?" Charley handed it to her. She pulled a jeweler's loupe out of a net bag hanging on the back of her chair and put it up to the photo. "Yes, I think you're right. I noticed his suit at the gala, too—blue and white stripes. Perhaps a bit too early in the season for seersucker, but a classic."

She held the photo out to Bethany, who placed it in the second position.

"So he was alive then. And the rest of these all show Amara at the table. You can see they span the night. I told you, she didn't leave my side until she got that phone call, and that was near the end."

Charley leaned over to get a better look at the pictures. "How can you tell these pictures spanned the night? They all look the same."

Bethany pointed to each photo in turn. "Look at the stacks of cups. They get shorter and shorter as more people eat the chowder. In this one, they're almost gone, and Amara is still there."

"That doesn't mean she didn't shoot him after this one was taken." Charley sat back and crossed her arms.

"Scone?" Fancy asked, and passed a rose-patterned plate across the table.

"No thanks, we just had lunch," Bethany said, and nudged the plate toward Charley. The china pinged against the fork at Charley's place setting. Bethany froze. *The noise.* "Why didn't we hear the gunshot?"

"What?"

"Why didn't we hear the gunshot? The one that killed Todd?"

Charley shrugged. "I don't know. It was a small gun."

"But it happened inside the bell tower, which is designed to *amplify* noise, not muffle it. Why didn't we hear it?" Bethany drummed her fingers on the tabletop. "Did you hear it, Fancy?"

"Me?" Fancy looked taken aback, as though she didn't expect to be included in the conversation.

"Yes. You were there, too. Did you hear anything that sounded like a gunshot? Fireworks, a car backfiring, any kind of loud noise?"

Fancy shook her head. "Only the church bells."

Bethany gasped.

"What?" Charley looked puzzled. "Todd rang the bells, right? So he was alive then."

"What if he was shot while he was ringing the bells? And the bells hid the sound of the gun?"

Charley nodded. "That makes a lot of sense. Nobody saw him after that, right?"

"Right. It seemed like everyone was looking for him, but no one had seen him. That's why I was sure he'd gone home to change his clothes! He's not the type to miss his own party. He must have been laying there, bleeding out, for most of the gala." Bethany's hand quivered as she arranged the photographs into a single stack.

Fancy's typical pallor took on a green tinge, and she wavered a bit, as though she were about to faint. Charley pushed back her chair and stood up.

"I'm so sorry," she said. "This isn't really appropriate talk for teatime. My apologies, Ms. Peters. We got carried away. These photos are so helpful, though. I'm afraid I have to take them into evidence."

Fancy nodded, blotting her forehead with a handkerchief. "Be my guest. I have the negatives."

Bethany picked up the stack of photographs and handed them to Charley. Turning to Fancy, she said, "Just out of curiosity, why didn't you take any photos inside the church? I remember you saying you were trying to make a record of the architectural detail, but all the pictures are of the exterior."

Fancy put her hand to her chest, her fingertips fluttering. "I did, early on in the evening. Unfortunately, none of the photographs were useful as souvenirs. I only printed the ones I thought would be interesting to tourists."

Bethany frowned. "You printed plenty of the food table."

Fancy ducked her head apologetically. "Those were for the newspaper. Robin asked me for them."

"I'd like to take a look at them," Charley said. "The interior photos. They may have clues about who was inside the church and when."

"I'll print them for you and drop them by the station." Fancy motioned weakly. "Shall I see you out?"

Charley nodded and headed back down the dim hallway to the front door. Bethany followed behind. They stepped out onto the porch, and Charley thanked Fancy for her hospitality.

But just as she was heading down the steps to the front walk, Bethany turned back to Fancy. "Why don't you just give Charley—Officer Perez—the negatives right now? It'll save you a lot of work."

"I don't mind. I'm happy to help." She smiled and closed the door.

"She's strange," Bethany said as they walked to the car.

Charley held up the bag of photographs. "But she might have just proven Amara is innocent."

Chapter 26

Friday

"Took you long enough!" Coop said.

Bethany grinned. To be honest, she'd forgotten about him while she was inside Fancy's house. She'd been so absorbed by examining the photos that she hadn't given Coop a second thought.

"Sorry not sorry," Charley said, tossing him the bag of photos. "Got these. I think we can put together a solid timeline of everyone's movements using the photos of the gala. Plus she's going to bring more by the station."

"Today?" Coop asked as he thumbed through the photos. He seemed to have sobered up during his wait in the car.

Charley shook her head. "She didn't say when. I'm sure it'll be today or tomorrow, though."

Bethany frowned. *It could be longer. And who knows how many nasty articles about me will be printed in the paper by then.* "It might be days before she prints the photos—or weeks! I really think you should get the negatives now."

"She's got a point." Coop twisted in his seat to look at Bethany approvingly.

"I already told her she could bring them into the station," Charley said, clearly annoyed. "Just because I'm a junior officer doesn't mean I don't know what I'm doing!"

Coop held up his hands defensively. "Fine, no need to jump down my throat. I just want to catch bad guys here."

"So do I." Charley turned the key and slammed the squad car into gear. "I'm taking you home now, Bethany."

They were silent for the rest of the ride to the cottage. Charley got out and walked Bethany to the door.

Bethany put her key in the lock and then paused. "I'm sorry I undermined you in front of Coop."

Charley shook her head and stuffed her hands in her pockets. "It's OK. You weren't wrong. If Fancy doesn't bring the pictures in today or tomorrow morning, I'll go get the negatives from her. Hopefully the pictures will help solve Todd's murder."

"Good luck, Charley." Bethany turned the key and pushed open the door.

"Wait." Charley glanced over her shoulder at the squad car. Coop wasn't looking their direction. He was bouncing and shaking his shoulders and bopping his head. Charley rolled her eyes. "Must have the radio on. Anyway, could you tell Kimmy something for me when you see her again?"

Bethany nodded. "Sure."

"Tell her I'm doing everything I can to solve both these crimes. I'm convinced that Amara didn't commit arson *or* murder, but it might take a little while to convince everyone else."

Bethany nodded again. "I understand. I'll tell her."

Chapter 27

Kimmy popped a Cheeto in her mouth. "Guess what! I talked to Olive. She said she was *very* interested in having you work at the bakery."

Bethany winced. "I know she's your friend and everything, but it's only a counter job. I really want to cook."

"That's just it! She hadn't really considered hiring a real chef, but the more she thought about it, the more she realized she could use help with the baking as well as the counter. So she wanted me to tell you that if you want to bake, she'll make the position fifty-fifty."

"Wow, really? How nice of her."

Kimmy nodded. "Nice is the name of her game. You should go down and apply for real."

"But it's still only for the summer, right? And part-time." Bethany sighed. "I guess something is better than nothing—and I do want to learn how to bake. Do you think Olive's heard what people are saying about me? She might not want that kind of attention for the Honor Roll."

"She heard, but she doesn't believe the gossip. Plus, I'm vouching for you, and she's known me since I was a kid. You should go talk to her in the morning. The bakery's open on Saturdays even though the train station is closed. You want ice cream?" Kimmy asked as she headed for the kitchen. Bethany nodded, and Kimmy got out two bowls. She retrieved a tub of from the freezer and jammed a spoon into the top of the chocolate ice cream. It wouldn't budge even when she leaned on the spoon with all her weight.

"Maybe give that a minute to thaw." Bethany grinned. "I meant to say—you know Charley, the cop? She wanted me to tell you that she doesn't think Amara killed Todd."

Kimmy stopped in mid-scoop. "She doesn't? She actually said that?"

"Yup. She said she is working as hard as she can to find the real criminals, and she wanted you to know. I think she likes you."

Kimmy rolled her eyes. "She's literally doing her job. Do you want people thinking you have the hots for them because you make them a good bowl of chowder?"

"I dunno. She waited until we were out of earshot of her partner to say it. It'd be like me taking a diner aside to say, 'Hey, tell your friend I made sure to slice her tomato *perfectly*.' It's not normal."

Kimmy wrestled the ice cream into submission and returned to the couch with two bowls and two spoons. She handed one to Bethany and sank into the sofa with a sigh of relief. "Why do you think she told you that, then? I mean, besides your ridiculous theory about her interest in me. She must be pretty confident about Auntie's innocence."

"Well, first off, Fancy's photos put Todd at Amara's house on Sunday evening. It's looking likely that he is the one who set the fire. We also were able to piece together a rough timeline of what happened at the gala using photos of the food service table. It's pretty clear that Amara didn't leave the table until late in the party, when Todd was already—well, you know."

Bethany soothed the lump in her throat with an extra-large spoonful of ice cream.

"Maybe we should crack open some champagne to go with this!" Kimmy grinned.

Hard to feel celebratory when Todd's murderer is still at large.

Bethany gave a half-hearted smile. "Let's save the champagne for when Charley finds the real killer."

Kimmy put her hand on Bethany's arm. "You're right. I'm sorry. I know this must be tough for you, too."

Bethany nodded and scooped up the last couple bites of her ice cream. "Yum. That was just what I needed. You done?"

Kimmy gobbled the dregs of her bowl and handed it to Bethany, who took the dishes to the sink.

"Did Charley say when Auntie can come home?'

"No, not yet. First they have to figure out who had the opportunity to kill Todd. They're going to make a detailed outline of everyone's movements at the gala using the photos Fancy gave us, plus some more she hasn't printed yet. They're of the interior of the church, and Charley thinks there could be something on them."

"Did they get the negatives?"

Bethany shook her head. "She's going to print them some copies. Charley said if she doesn't bring them to the station by tomorrow morning, she'll go ask for the negatives."

Kimmy's mouth dropped open in disbelief. "Do you trust her?"

"To get the negatives? Of course, that's her job."

"I mean Fancy, not Charley. You haven't seen the other film, right? Anything could be on it. What if she destroys it? Or doesn't print all the photos?"

Bethany tilted her head. "Charley trusts her, I guess. And she seems pretty wimpy to have murdered Todd. She didn't even have the stomach for our conversation about it."

"Even if she didn't, maybe it was someone she knew, though. Someone she liked and wanted to protect. She might try to help them by destroying the evidence."

Dread crept up Bethany's spine. She didn't want to believe Kimmy's theory, but she had to admit that it wasn't crazy, either. If Fancy realized that Todd had burned down Amara's house to get the development approved, she'd have been furious—maybe even angry enough to look the other way when someone wanted him dead.

"We have to go get those negatives right now," Kimmy said, sitting up straight. "If the negatives disappear, so does Auntie's chance at being proven innocent."

"Slow down. What's you're suggesting is illegal! We can't just break in and take stuff, even if it's evidence of a crime."

"It's worth it if it means Auntie doesn't spend the rest of her life in jail." Kimmy stuck out her jaw stubbornly. "I'm going. You can come with me or you can stay here—your choice."

Bethany sighed. "I'm coming with you—if only to keep *you* out of jail."

Chapter 28

Kimmy parked the Honda across the street and a few houses down from Fancy's teal gingerbread Victorian. "And I thought the swan porch was bad," she muttered under her breath.

"I'm sure those colors are period." Bethany grinned and scratched Sharky behind the ears. "We can watch her place from here. The negatives are definitely in the darkroom, so as long as she doesn't go in there, we know they're safe. In the morning, we'll accidentally run into her as she's going out to print the photos and ask if she'll show us how she does it."

"What if she does go in there tonight? Then what?"

"Then we'll release the hounds!" Bethany pretended to open the car door for Sharky.

"Seriously. She might have already damaged them, or thrown them away. She might be in there right now!"

"Look." Bethany pointed up at a second-story window on Fancy's house. A figured was silhouetted behind lace curtains. "She's headed to bed. That means *we* can go to bed and come back at the crack of dawn to make sure she turns over all the negatives to the police. We can even call Charley to come with us. I'm sure she wouldn't mind seeing *you*."

Kimmy pursed her lips. "I'd rather stay here. Just to be sure."

"Fine." Bethany sighed. Sharky whined and pawed at the door. "No. Lay down."

Sharky stared at her belligerently and pawed at the door again.

"Stop it! Be a good boy."

Sharky launched himself at the door handle in one final desperate attempt to get out, and to Bethany's horror, it succeeded. The door opened a crack, just large enough for a medium-sized chihuahua to jump out of the car and run down the street.

Bethany and Kimmy both stared at each other, frozen, and then leaped out of the car after the dog. Sharky yipped a them and ran a little farther toward Fancy's house, stopping to raise a leg and pee on a shrub out front.

"Sharky, come!" Kimmy hissed, patting her knees. Sharky looked over his shoulder at her, but kept running in the opposite direction.

Bethany scrambled in the backseat of the car for his leash. "Sharky? Want to go on a walkie with Bethany?" She shook the leash so the clip jangled. Sharky skidded to a halt and his ears perked up. She shook it again. "Walkie time?"

She took a few steps toward him, smiling and holding out the leash. He barked and scampered a few yards toward her, then eyed her suspiciously.

"Let's go for a walk!"

He leaped joyfully and bolted toward her. When he reached her, she caught his collar with her left hand and deftly attached the leash with her right, then let out a huge sigh of relief and sat down on the sidewalk next to the dog.

"Oh, thank god," Kimmy said, still loud-whispering. "You got him." She took the leash out of Bethany's hand and started for the car.

Bethany waved her hands to stop her. "Wait. You have to actually take him on a walk now, or next time he won't come to you. Dog training 101."

Kimmy raised an eyebrow skeptically. "How do you know so much about dog training?"

Bethany giggled. "A dog training program hosted by that guy Alvar Alcomb comes on right after my favorite cooking show. Guilty pleasure."

"Is he the one that People Magazine voted Sexiest Man Alive last year?"

"Yup. That's the one. Sexiest celebrity dog trainer alive."

Kimmy grinned. "No wonder you didn't turn off the TV." She glanced down the road toward Fancy's house. "I guess I'll just take Sharky on a little spin, then."

"No! You're not doing what I think you're doing..."

Kimmy blinked innocently. "I'm just taking my little dog for a walk like you told me to."

Darn you, Alvar Alcomb. And you, too, Sharky. Bethany scrambled to her feet and trotted after Kimmy toward Fancy's house.

"Listen, you can't steal evidence! It could make it inadmissible in court. You need a warrant and stuff." Bethany jogged to catch up.

"Just because you got into law school doesn't mean you're suddenly a legal expert." Kimmy gave her the side-eye and pulled out her phone. She selected a number and put the phone to her ear. "Hi, Charley? This is Kimmy Caldwell. Fine, thanks. I was wondering—if a civilian performs a search of private property, does he or she need a search warrant for any evidence found to be admissible in court? Oh, no, of course I wouldn't. I'm just curious. Thank you."

She ended the call and turned triumphantly to Bethany. "Trespassing is illegal, but it doesn't make evidence inadmissible. So there. I'm going to get those negatives." She checked to make sure the street was clear and headed across Fancy's lawn toward the darkroom shed, Sharky at her heels.

"Stop!" Bethany yell-whispered, but Kimmy didn't even glance in her direction, so she ran to catch up. "At least hear me out. I know where Fancy keeps the key. We can go in, *look* at the negatives, make sure they're all there, then leave. We are not going to steal stuff. You know Amara would kill you herself if you did, and I'll tell her!"

"It's not fair to use her against me!" Kimmy put her hands on her hips. "Anyway, what if Fancy destroys them after we look at them?"

"If there's anything in the negatives, we'll take pictures of them, OK?"

Kimmy nodded. "Fine. Where's the key?"

Bethany pointed to a flowerbed near the entrance to the darkroom. "Under the little squirrel statue."

Kimmy bent to lift the statue and find the key. After she replaced the squirrel in its original position, Sharky lifted his leg and peed on it. "Nice," she said, and patted him on the head. He immediately began digging in the flowerbed, sending a spray of dirt flying out behind him.

Bethany looked up at the second-story windows on Fancy's house. The windows were dark now. Fancy must have gone to bed. Kimmy unlocked the darkroom door and started to go inside, but Bethany put her hand on her arm.

"Wait—you can't take Sharky in there. He's filthy! Plus he'll probably chew on something he's not supposed to."

"Well, I can't leave him out here alone! He'll just bark and wake up everyone on the block!" Kimmy whispered.

"You stay out here with Sharky and keep watch for Fancy and any nosy neighbors. I'll look at the negatives and take pictures of any that seem incriminating, just in case. You give the signal if someone is coming."

Kimmy sighed. "Fine. What's the signal? Hoot like an owl?"

Bethany giggled. "I think that will look pretty suspicious if you're standing around someone's yard doing bird calls. Maybe just say 'bad dog!'"

Kimmy grinned at Sharky. The dog looked at her and scratched an ear with his hind leg. "OK, go! The longer we stand here, the more likely it is that someone's going to notice!"

Bethany nodded and stepped into the darkroom, carefully closing the door behind her before turning on the light switch. The red bulb glowed dimly, but her eyes adjusted in just a few moments and she could see the layout of the room. It was a small space but efficiently designed. Several work benches lined the walls, and a sink and developing station were set up at the far end. In the center of the room, a work table held an enlarger and a light table. A string of drying photographs was stretched across the back wall. Bethany crossed to them immediately.

Pictures of the church interior. Fancy must have printed them after she and Charley left. Bethany counted fifteen photos, which didn't seem like many to document the entire interior of the church—and none of them showed the interior of the bell tower where Todd was killed.

Maybe it was locked and she couldn't access that area. Or maybe...

"Where are the negatives?" Bethany mumbled aloud. She looked around. A tall metal cabinet stood to her right. She tried the door, but it was locked.

Odd. She looked around for the key, but it wasn't hanging on the wall or in the dish of odds and ends by the sink.

"Bad dog!"

Bethany dove underneath the work table and wrapped her arms around her knees, trying to shrink into the smallest space possible. She held her breath and strained her ears to hear what was going on outside.

Kimmy's voice came through the door. "Sorry, false alarm. Sharky tried to eat my purse."

Bethany let out her breath in a rush and unfolded her limbs as she tried scooting out from under the table.

Funny how it's always harder to get out than it is to get in.

She banged her head sharply. *Ouch.* When she reached up to feel the bump, the back of her hand brushed something stuck to the bottom of the tabletop above her head.

The key. It was attached to a magnetic holder underneath the table. Bethany stood up, felt under the table for the key, and tried it in the cabinet. The door opened easily and her heart leaped. Inside were neat rows of storage boxes, some labeled with dates and others with subject matter. Bethany scanned them, looking for a label she recognized. July 2016, Society Meetings, Newbridge Station—and Hosanna Street!

She slid the box from the shelf. It was heavier than she expected. Fancy must have been taking photos on Hosanna Street for a while. She put the box on the work table and flicked through the envelopes of negatives inside. Again, each was neatly labeled. If Fancy ever got tired of running her souvenir shop, she certainly had a career waiting for her at the Newbridge Public Library.

She pulled out the envelope marked "Gala" and spread the negatives on the light table. She flicked it on and squinted at the negatives, trying to make out the images, but they were so small and in reversed colors that she struggled with each one.

Her shoulders tensed. This was taking far too much time. She remembered the tool Fancy had used to look at the photos that afternoon, and quickly scanned the darkroom for a similar item. She spied an identical net bag hanging on the wall and fished a loupe out of it.

Success! But her heart sank when she used it to view the negatives. They were all the same pictures she'd seen earlier. Fancy seemed to have printed all of the negatives from the party and exterior of the church. Bethany slid them back into the envelope and stuck it back into the box.

Where were the negatives of the church interior?

She flicked through the box of Hosanna Street photos again. Some envelopes were marked with last names. *Maybe the names of homeowners?* Just out of curiosity, Bethany pulled out the envelope marked "Caldwell," and put those negatives on the light table.

The first few frames were exterior shots of Amara's house from different angles. They seemed to have been taken before Amara built the porch addition. As she moved through the film, strip-by-strip, the photos changed. Some documented the porch construction, from foundation to painting. Then a few strips showed the completed swan porch, some taken close up and some from further away—down the street or in neighbor's yards.

Amara must have kicked her off the property. Bethany grinned. She moved the loupe to the last strip of negatives and froze.

The fire.

Fancy had taken actual photographs of the fire that burned down Amara's house.

Bethany swallowed hard. The first picture showed the flames when they'd barely started and were just licking the railings on the porch itself. That meant that Fancy had to have seen who lit the fire. The last photo showed the fire consuming the lower half of the entire house. Amara and Sharky have still been inside the house when it was taken. Bethany got chills just like she had when she'd seen the picture of the church bell tower that had Todd's lifeless body inside.

Did Fancy just let it burn? Or was she the one who called 9-1-1?

She fumbled in her pocket for her phone and tried to focus it on the light table. The phone camera balked for a moment, and then the images became clear and Bethany hit the shutter button. She jammed the phone back in her pocket and scooped up the negatives with one hand, sliding them back into the envelope. She tucked the envelope back into the box and riffled through the remaining envelopes to see if any of the negatives of the church interior were stashed there.

Nada.

She sighed and slid the box back onto the shelf. None of the other boxes had promising labels.

Maybe Fancy took the negatives of the church interior into the house.

She closed the cabinet and turned the key.

"Bad dog!"

Bethany dove underneath the worktable again.

"What are you doing in my yard?" Fancy's voice was muffled, but loud enough that Bethany could understand every word.

"Just walking my *bad dog* Sharky," Kimmy said. "He ran over here and I just caught him."

"I know you." Fancy's voice was louder and more threatening. "You're Amara Caldwell's girl. What are you doing in *this* neighborhood?"

"Just walking my dog, ma'am." Bethany could tell Kimmy was angry. Her voice was tight and unnaturally even.

Bethany heard Fancy gasp. "Where's my key?! Did you go into my darkroom!"

"Ma'am, I—"

"I'm calling the police!"

"I didn't take anything, I swear! I just came to get my dog. See? I don't have any of your stuff. Maybe you forgot to put the key away."

"You wait right there. If you run off, or if I find one thing out of place, I'm calling 9-1-1."

Bethany heard the sound of the darkroom doorknob turning. She squeezed her eyes shut and cursed herself for not locking the door behind her.

Fancy entered, carrying an old-fashioned lamp that lit up the small shed.

Kerosene. Bethany's heart thudded in her chest. Maybe Fancy hadn't just seen the arsonist. Maybe she *was* the arsonist. But why would she burn down Amara's house if it meant the neighborhood lost its historic designation? It didn't make sense.

Fancy set the lamp down near the sink and stood so close to the table that her long skirt blocked Bethany's view momentarily. Fancy reached under the table and Bethany leaned back so her fingers wouldn't brush her face.

Why didn't I take the key out of the cabinet when I hid? Bethany gritted her teeth.

Fancy felt around for the key, and then, when she didn't find it, ducked down to look under the table. Her eyes met Bethany's and went wide with shock.

"What are you doing here?!" she cried. She grabbed Bethany by the hair and dragged her out from under the table. Bethany's scalp screamed and she couldn't help but follow Fancy's motions.

"I was just...curious...about your...pictures," Bethany panted, holding onto her hair with both hands so Fancy wouldn't pull it out by the roots. Fancy let go and pushed her back against the wall, and Bethany choked back a sob. "My boyfriend was murdered, and I didn't know what else to do. I was hoping you had something on film that would help solve the case!"

Fancy narrowed her eyes. "Why didn't you just knock on the door and ask? We're acquainted—I might have shown you what I had."

Bethany's mind whirred trying to come up with a believable lie. "I was trying to work up the nerve to ask, but that lady out there came by with her dog, and I panicked and ran in here to hide!"

Fancy relaxed a little. "Maybe I forgot to lock up this evening."

At that, Bethany relaxed a little bit, too. She eyed the door, wondering if she could dash for the exit and get to Kimmy's car in time.

I hope Kimmy's out there warming it up.

"Did you set this darkroom up yourself? It's really cool." To her own ears, Bethany's voice sounded brittle and sycophantic, but Fancy blinked in surprise.

"Yes, I did. Photography has long been a hobby of mine." She smiled a little. "Does it interest you?"

"Sure." Bethany nodded and Fancy raised her eyebrows. Flattery seemed to be working to soften her, so Bethany laid on a bit more. "It seems complicated, though—all the equipment and chemistry."

"It's not, once you get used to it. It's mostly just measurements and doing things in the right order. You're a caterer, right?"

"Chef," Bethany said automatically.

"Well, it's much like following a recipe. One part developer to fifty parts water, and so forth."

"That doesn't sound so bad." Bethany smiled, but behind the smile her mind was pacing in circles, frantically looking for a way out of the tiny shed.

"What pictures did you want to see?" Fancy asked suddenly.

"Inside the church?" Bethany said lamely. "I hoped there would be a clue who might have followed Todd into the bell tower."

Fancy motioned to the damp photos hanging on the wire. "They're all up here. Go ahead and look at them. I'm taking them into the police tomorrow."

Bethany gingerly began examining the photos that she'd already looked at, keeping one eye on Fancy. "Hm. I don't see anything. Is this all of them?"

Fancy crossed her arms and leaned against the cabinet. "Yes, of course."

"I just thought—well, I thought maybe you took more. This doesn't seem like very many."

"The others were no good. Out of focus, light leaks, and so forth." Fancy waved her hand. "I think it's about time you leave."

"You should take the negatives to the police, too," Bethany babbled, as Fancy herded her toward the door. Fancy snorted. "Really—they might be able to extract something from them. Even if the photos themselves are bad, they might have good content." She paused, thinking. "Unless you're hiding something."

Fancy stopped, grabbed her by the elbow, and spun her around. "What did you see? Have you been meddling in my cupboard?" She looked over at the cabinet and saw the key still sticking out of the lock. "You *have*, haven't you?"

She reached into the pocket of her bathrobe and withdrew a small pistol and pointed it at Bethany.

Bethany drew in her breath. *It's exactly like the one I found in the chowder!*

Fancy seemed to read her mind. "My father had a pair of Brownings. I'm sorry to have lost the other one."

"So you—" Bethany began, realization dawning.

"He was going to destroy this town! Hosanna Street first, but then he'd go on to another project, and another!" Fancy waved the pistol wildly, and Bethany ducked out of instinct. "I have Amara to thank, really—if she hadn't thrown food all over him, I'd never have had the opportunity to stop him once and for all."

Please, Kimmy, call the police. With a sinking stomach, Bethany realized that even if Kimmy had called Charley, it could be some time before the she arrived.

I've got to keep her talking.

"You wanted to punish him for the arson?"

Fancy's eyes narrowed and her cheeks flushed. "Didn't you see the photographs?"

"I saw some pictures of the fire. I thought maybe you saw who set it. It didn't make sense to me that you'd burn down Amara's house, knowing that it would mean the development would go forward! But"—she glanced at the kerosene lamp by the sink—"maybe I was wrong."

"It wasn't supposed to burn the whole house!" Fancy's arm shook as she pointed the gun at Bethany. "Just the ridiculous swan head on the porch! But it got too big, too fast. I called the fire department—I didn't want to hurt anyone. I stayed until they came to make sure Amara got out alive."

Bethany nodded as she tried to keep her breathing even. That explained the tracks behind George's shed. Fancy must have parked her tricycle there so it wouldn't be seen. "You wanted the porch gone so there'd be no way the city council would approve the development, even six months or a year down the line."

Fancy smiled. Her teeth glinted in the lamplight, and Bethany shivered. Her smile was even more ominous than her frown. "That's right. And I'd already made an agreement with Don Hefferman for the historical society to purchase the old church property. I just didn't expect—" Her face clouded, but she shook it off. "I had to make things right. I wasn't sure how. I brought one of my father's pistols to the gala. I didn't want to hurt anyone, but I thought..."

Bethany tried to use a sympathetic tone. "You thought you could threaten Todd and make things go back to the way they were before the arson."

Fancy lowered the gun slightly. "Yes, thank you. Someone who understands. I confronted him as he was going into the bell tower, and I asked him nicely to call off the development. I followed him up the stairs, explaining all the reasons why it was a bad idea! I thought he was listening to me, but then he said the show must go on and started ringing the bells! So I—"

"Shot him," Bethany finished. "And then dumped the pistol in my soup so I'd get blamed."

Fancy pulled the gun up and pointed it at Bethany again. "It wasn't *like* that." She took a step closer. "If he'd just have *listened* to me, we wouldn't be in this mess."

Bethany put her hands up and moved backward until she bumped against a workbench. "Please, you don't have to do this!"

Fancy didn't seem to hear her. "Shame about all my equipment," she murmured, scanning the room. "I'll mourn the loss of all my negatives, too, but I suppose it can't be helped. Turn around and put your hands behind your back!"

Bethany obeyed, panic welling in her chest, and felt Fancy bind her wrists with some kind of tape. "You won't get away with this! The police are already on their way!"

Please let them be on their way. She turned around. Fancy had put away her gun and was standing by the door, holding the kerosene lamp.

She smiled sweetly at Bethany. "I'll be sure to let them know that you confessed to killing your boyfriend because you were angry at him for setting the fire. You broke into my shed to destroy evidence of your guilt, but when I confronted you, you knocked the lamp out of my hand and set the place on fire by accident."

She pushed open the door and held up the lamp.

"No, wait!" Bethany lunged toward her, but pulled up short as Fancy let go of the lamp and it crashed to the floor.

A fireball rose up between them, and Bethany only had time to see the door close behind Fancy before she lost consciousness.

Chapter 29

Someone was banging on the door. Bethany's eyes fluttered open, and Kimmy's concerned face came into focus.

"You feeling up to visitors?" she asked. "It's already after noon."

Bethany sat up and twisted her hair into a bun. She stifled a yawn. "Yeah, I'm OK. Let them in."

Kimmy came back with Charley and Coop in tow. The two officers had worried expressions, but they fell away as they saw Bethany sitting on the sofa.

"I'm fine, guys!" She stood up and twirled around. "Not a single burn, thanks to you. The ER doctor said the damage from the smoke inhalation was minimal, too. I just passed out because the initial blast used up all the oxygen in the shed."

"It's a good thing Kimmy called us right away. We got there just in time." Charley sank into one of the armchairs. Coop took a seat in the other, and Sharky jumped up into his lap.

He chuckled. "Hey, little guy."

"We came to take your statement." Charley held up her clipboard. "We have most of the details already, but we have some things to confirm with you."

Bethany's heart raced as she wondered what Fancy had told them. *How am I going to prove I didn't kill Todd?* "I don't even know how to use a gun," she said awkwardly, and she felt her cheeks flush.

Kimmy put her hand on Bethany's arm. "Relax. I heard everything Fancy said—I had my ear to the wall the whole time. And Charley and Coop arrived just as Fancy lit up the shed. They know she's responsible for the arson *and* the murder."

Bethany sighed with relief.

"We arrested her last night, and she was charged this morning with both crimes." Charley smiled reassuringly. "We still have to collect evidence for the court case, though. Unfortunately the darkroom was totally destroyed. Do you remember anything you saw in there that night that you'd be willing to testify about?"

"I remember what I *didn't* see," Bethany said. "She had fifteen prints made of the church interior, but the negatives were nowhere to be found. I think she may have taken them inside the house."

"Nice," Coop said. "Maybe we'll find them when we do a search."

"Anything else that might be incriminating?" Charley asked. "Besides the kerosene lamp—we already know about that."

"Speaking of the kerosene, she had negatives of Amara's house burning down! She basically documented the whole thing, right up until the fire department arrived." Bethany felt her pockets and then looked around the room. "Did my phone make it out of there?"

"Oh! Yes!" Kimmy ran to get her purse from the hook by the door. She opened it and took out the phone. "It's fine. It was still in your pocket when you got to the hospital."

She handed the phone to Bethany, who pulled up the photos of the negatives. She zoomed in and gave the phone to Charley.

"See? The first photo is when the fire had just started, and then the last is when the house was totally consumed." Bethany pointed to the photos as Charley scrolled through them.

Kimmy's hand flew to her mouth. "I don't think I can even look at those," she said, tears springing to her eyes.

Bethany put an arm around her shoulders and squeezed. "Amara can rebuild it exactly as it was, now that she's off the hook for the arson and can collect the insurance money."

"These are great. Really great," Charley said, handing the phone back. "I sent them to myself so you don't need to come down to the station."

"I hope I never have to go to the police station again." Kimmy grimaced. "No offense, but I've had enough law enforcement this week to last the rest of my life."

Coop chuckled. "You might want to come down there, though, if only to see Perez's new luxury suite."

Charley grimaced. "What he *means* is that I got promoted to detective and am moving to a new office. It's only a little bigger."

"Wow, congratulations!" Kimmy said, her face lighting up.

"Was it because of this case?" Bethany asked. Charley nodded. "You're welcome, then! That's almost worth getting blown up for."

"Yeah, I owe you both a drink." Charley smiled broadly.

"I owe *you* one," Kimmy said. "For keeping my auntie out of jail. You really listened to us and believed us."

"Well, when this case is closed, I'd love to take you up on that," Charley said.

Bethany grinned at Kimmy. "She'd love to take you up on that," she repeated.

Coop cracked up, and his laughter made Sharky bark.

"I heard," Kimmy said, looking at the floor in embarrassment. "I'd like that, too."

Charley got to her feet, biting her lip to hold back a smile. "Come on, Coop, we have everything we need."

"Perez is calling the shots now!" Coop gave Sharky a final pat and set him down on the floor. "We'll be in touch if we need anything else."

"Call me," Charley added, looking at Kimmy. "I'm there if you need me.

"Got it." Kimmy held up her phone. "I'll let you know when my aunt arrives in town."

Bethany closed the door behind the cops and leaned against it. She squealed quietly. "I think you have a girlfriend!"

Kimmy rolled her eyes, but she couldn't stop smiling. "One date does not a girlfriend make. I owe her one for saving our lives—after that, we'll see."

"She's cute, Kimmy. I have a good feeling about her."

Kimmy giggled and then pursed her lips, pretending to disapprove. "I *said* we'll see."

"When does Amara's train get in?" Bethany clicked on her phone to check the time. *One o'clock—and seven missed calls from Mom while the phone was in Kimmy's purse.* She sighed. She was going to have to face that music sooner or later.

"Not until three. Want to come with me to welcome her home?"

Bethany nodded. "We should bring this little guy, too!" She nudged Sharky with her foot so he'd stop gnawing on the coffee table. "If only so he doesn't ruin another piece of furniture."

Kimmy looked around the room. "I'm not sure there's anything in here he hasn't customized!"

"This is why we can't have nice things," Bethany said solemnly. She scooped up Sharky and snuggled him. "I'm gonna miss you when you've gone back home, though." She jerked her head up to look at Kimmy. "*Not* that I want them to move in permanently."

Kimmy waved her hand and giggled. "Of course not. A week longer, tops. Hey, are you hungry? Want some lunch?"

Bethany's stomach growled at the mention of food. "Yeah, my hospital hot cereal has definitely worn off. What's on the menu?"

"I don't know—what are you going to make?" Kimmy wiggled her eyebrows.

Bethany lobbed a throw pillow at her. "*We* are going to make some quick omelets, and then *we* are going to bake cookies for Amara's welcome home."

Kimmy grinned. "I like how you think."

Chapter 30

As soon as Amara walked off the train, Kimmy let go of Sharky's leash. The dog bounded toward Amara, who opened her arms. Sharky leaped into them and licked her chin until she set him down and grabbed the end of his leash.

"My darlings!" she boomed, holding her arms out toward Kimmy and Bethany. Bethany smiled and stepped back as Amara embraced Kimmy, but Amara pulled her into the hug, too. "It is so good to be home!"

"It's good to have you back," Kimmy said fervently. "We made cookies!"

Amara let go of them to look at the box of still-warm cookies Kimmy held. "Wonderful, no chocolate," she said, and tossed one to Sharky. He stopped gnawing on the corner of her suitcase and sat down with the cookie between his paws. Amara took one for herself and then motioned for Bethany and Kimmy to do the same.

Bethany bit into the cookie and it felt like being hugged all over again. The shortbread cookie melted and spread out over her tongue, and she smelled the warm perfume of orange zest and vanilla.

"Is this your recipe?" Amara asked Kimmy, brushing the crumbs from her embroidered wrap.

Kimmy shook her head. "Bethany's."

Amara looked Bethany up and down. "At least she can do one thing right! Mm, these are good." She popped another cookie in her mouth.

206

Amara is back in top form, I see. Bethany pasted on a smile. "Thanks."

"Let's get out of here." Kimmy handed the cookies to Bethany and picked up the suitcase, heading for the exit. Bethany followed, and Amara limped behind with Sharky.

"Slow down, child. These old bones can't keep up."

"Sorry, Auntie. I'm just excited to have you home." Kimmy paused while she waited for them to catch up.

"I don't know if I can ever go home," Amara wheezed. "Not now."

Kimmy looped her free arm through Amara's and patted her hand as they resumed walking. "Well, the arson case is solved, so you'll get your insurance money soon. Then you can find somewhere else to live, or you can rebuild the house just like it was. You'll have the choice."

Amara stopped again. "I do love my neighborhood. I missed it while I was at Pearl's. Maybe I will rebuild after all. Ol' Sharky and I can bunk with you until it's done."

Bethany involuntarily made a face. Kimmy looked over her shoulder and grinned at her. "Oh, I think we'll find you a little place to stay that's all your own, so you can spread out and be comfortable. How does that sound?"

Amara nodded and started walking toward the exit again. "That sounds just fine."

Bethany chuckled to herself. On the way out, they passed the Honor Roll, and she noticed the help-wanted sign was still in the window. "Hey, do you mind if I stop in the bakery to talk to Olive? I'll just be a minute."

Kimmy waved. "We'll wait for you in the car!"

Bethany pushed through the swinging door into the bakery. Olive saw her immediately and gave her a floury wave.

"Did you talk to Kimmy?" she called across the room.

Bethany nodded and made her way to the counter. "She told me what you said about the job. I really appreciate that you rethought the position. I'd love to apply, even if it's just for the summer. I think it could be a good way for me to work while I get my catering business off the ground, plus I'd love to learn what you do here."

Olive gave a satisfied little sigh. "Perfect. You're hired. You come with the best references." She winked.

Bethany hesitated. "Do you—have you read the articles about me in the paper? Do you think that'll be a problem? The case has been solved and everything, but it might take a while to get sorted out in the public perception. People still think of me as the 'crime chowder' girl."

Olive smiled, her eyes twinkling. "I hope they'll soon start thinking of you as the bakery girl. The proof will be in the pudding."

"Or the evidence will be in the soup," Bethany joked. "Would you like one of my cookies? Kimmy and I made them this afternoon."

Olive nodded and reached for one. "Don't mind if I do. It's not often that I get to eat someone else's baking." As she tasted it, her face smoothed until she looked almost blissful.

"Do you like it?" Bethany asked eagerly.

Olive grinned. "You know—I think you're going to work out just fine here, bakery girl. You start on Monday."

Bethany left the bakery with a skip in her step. She had one thing left to do. She pulled her phone out and held it to her ear as she walked out to the car.

"Hi, Mom? I just wanted to catch you up on a few things."

Epilogue

"Thank you all for coming!" Olive said, clasping her hands together. The crowd that had gathered at the steps of the old church on Hosanna Street strained forward to hear her words. Bethany stood on a chair to see over the crowd from the food service table. "As the president of the Newbridge Historic Society, I'm thrilled to welcome you to the ribbon-cutting ceremony for our town museum and cultural center!"

The crowd clapped and cheered, but Bethany smiled sadly. Olive really was the perfect person to be the new president of the historical society—kind, fair, and well-versed in local history—but it was bittersweet that Todd's death made this happy scene possible.

I hope that, wherever he is, he's at peace.

"This will be a place for the whole town to gather and remember our past, and especially for this wonderful neighborhood, the heart of our community. I'll step aside so the new museum director can say a few words. Dr. Washington?"

George joined her on the steps. He wore a blue suit and a brown knit tie that looked straight out of the 1970s, back when he was a young history professor. Bethany hadn't known he was one of the leading scholars of African-American history when she met him, but Olive had quickly caught her up on his long and important career during their early-morning hours at the bakery. He'd been one of Olive's mentors when she studied history herself.

"Hello, folks," he said, giving a half-wave. "I guess this is it. We've been waiting a long time for something like this, and now we've got it, so it's up to us to make the brave people who founded this church—and this town—proud. I promise you that we'll get these doors open by the fall, so the school kids can visit. Mayor Strauss, if you'll do the honors?"

The mayor, who'd been awkwardly standing to the side holding a giant pair of golden shears, moved to the center of the stairs and positioned the scissors on the swash of red ribbon that was strung between the handrails. "All together, now!"

Olive and George each put a hand on the scissor handles, and the mayor heaved the scissors shut. The ribbon fell away, and the crowd cheered and clapped again.

Olive turned to face the crowd, her cheeks pink. "Refreshments in the back! Bethany made her famous chowder!"

The crowd broke up and Bethany scrambled down from the chair. She straightened her apron and started filling bowls of chowder as fast as she could, dotting the basil oil on top of each. Kimmy and Charley were some of the first people to the table. Bethany glanced up at them when they approached and smiled to herself.

Holding hands—that's a good sign.

"Couldn't stay away, huh?"

Charley grabbed two bowls and handed one to Kimmy. "No way. I wasn't sure I'd ever get to taste this again."

Kimmy took a bite and nodded. "It's really great. You've outdone yourself."

"Yep. No gun in this batch." Bethany grinned. Even she had to admit that this was even better than her chowder at the gala, now that she'd had time to perfect the balance of flavors—the sweet corn, salty clams, and earthy vegetables. And the basil oil was still the bright taste of summer on top. "Hopefully other people like it, too, and I'll pick up some catering gigs tonight!"

"You don't like your new gig as a baker?" Charley asked.

"Oh, I do—I just love cooking, too, and I'm not making enough money to even pay the rent!"

Kimmy shook her head. "Don't worry about that. I've got you covered for the next couple months while you figure everything out. Don't sweat it."

"Thank you." Bethany tried to smile through the tears that were threatening to fall in the soup. "I don't deserve friends like you."

Kimmy started to protest, but Bethany cut her off. "Now shoo, I need to get the rest of this soup out before it gets cold."

Charley swiped another bowl before she and Kimmy went to talk to Olive. Bethany groaned internally when she saw who was next in line. It was none other than Alex Vadecki. He must have come to gloat. But instead of a smug expression, he looked dour and uncomfortable as he picked up a bowl of chowder and a spoon from the table, his shoulders hunched and his forehead creased.

"Are you OK, Alex?" Bethany asked. "How's the franchise deal going?"

"What deal?" he said shortly, and shoveled soup into his mouth like he hadn't eaten since the gala. His face shifted as he tasted it. "Hey, this is great. Can I put it on the menu at the Grotto?"

"The deal with Don Hefferman. I know you signed the papers with him. Congratulations on the deal!"

He eyed her suspiciously. "What papers? The guy skipped town before he signed. Turned out he spent his money on something else—if he ever had any to begin with. I think he was just a con man, to be honest."

"But I saw them! They were—" Bethany stopped herself before she let on that she'd broken into Don's office. "Anyway, no, you can't have my chowder recipe. You'll just water it down."

Maybe Don signed the papers and then thought better of it. Maybe he tried the food!

She snickered in spite of herself.

"Sure, laugh about it. Thanks a lot." Alex sighed loudly. "You're still the same Bethany—you think you're better than everyone."

"Aw, come on. I don't think that. I'm really sorry it didn't work out for you this time. Don't give up on the idea, though." Bethany gave him a sympathetic smile as she filled her table with bowls of soup. No matter how quickly she ladled, she could barely keep up with the demand! "I bet there are other people here who might want to invest in a Grotto franchise. You should go mingle."

"You're right," he said, looking around the courtyard with a hopeful expression. "Thanks. Don't think this means I'll give you your job back, though."

"Bye, Alex," she said, rolling her eyes. But as he walked away, she felt a twinge of sadness to close the door on that chapter of her life.

"Bad blood between you two?" Robin Ricketts held her voice recorder out and seemed to have been eavesdropping for some time—long enough to figure out that Bethany and Alex had no love lost between them.

"No comment," Bethany said. "I've learned my lesson talking to you."

Robin clicked off the recorder and pretended to pout. "Aw, you don't like my stories?"

"Not really. Want some soup?"

Robin smiled and wrinkled her nose. "Not really."

"Well, that's all I'm serving here tonight, so..." Bethany made a walking motion with her two fingers.

Robin raised her eyebrows. "Suit yourself." She flounced off.

For a moment, Bethany felt a surge of dread as she thought about how Robin might spin their conversation in her next article. Then she looked nearby where Amara and George were chatting by the courtyard fountain, Sharky tangling them up in his leash. George was laughing so hard he was bent over.

"Not just a swan—I'm gonna put up a whole menagerie!" Amara declared, waving her arms dramatically, and George slapped his knee.

If they can mend fences, maybe there's hope for me and the Newbridge Community Observer. *Maybe not today or tomorrow, but eventually we'll play nice together.*

• • • •

HAPPY ENDING FOR HOSANNA STREET

By Robin Ricketts

Newbridge, CT—A museum and cultural center will highlight Newbridge's storied African-American history, giving a new voice to the town's founding citizens. The old Hosanna

Street church will house the new venture, slated to open in the fall.

The structure, which was originally scheduled to be demolished this week, will be preserved intact, says museum director George Washington. "We'll keep the character, but it might get some new plumbing!"

A ribbon-cutting ceremony for the museum was held by the historical society to celebrate the beginning of construction. Mayor Strauss, society president Olive Underwood, and Dr. Washington did the honors.

The celebration comes on the heels of the arrest and subsequent conviction of Fancy Peters, once president of the historical society and longtime proprietor of the souvenir kiosk at Newbridge Station, for the murder of Todd Luna. Luna formerly owned the church site and planned to raze it to make way for condominiums.

When asked if the city regretted the economic loss of the condominium development, the mayor replied, "The museum will bring in tourist dollars, and that's good for Newbridge, too."

The event was catered by Bethany Bradstreet, who declined to comment for this piece.

Recipes

Corn Chowder

C orn chowder is the perfect soup for almost any season. It's also the perfect base to add vegetables, meat, or seafood!

Ingredients

2 Tb butter
1 Tb olive oil
1 cup chopped onion
½ cup chopped celery
½ cup chopped carrots
1 Tb minced garlic (or ½ Tb garlic powder)
¼ cup flour
6 cups chicken or vegetable stock
2 cups cream or half-and-half
2 russet potatoes, peeled and diced
6 ears of corn (or 4-5 cups of canned or frozen corn)
Salt and pepper to taste
Basil or chive oil (see recipe)

Directions

Heat 2 Tbs butter and 1 Tb olive oil in a large pot over medium heat. Sautee the onion, celery, carrots, and garlic until soft. Add flour and stir to coat.

Add the stock and bring to a boil before adding the cream and diced potatoes. Boil for 7–8 minutes until the potatoes are very soft.

Slice the kernels from the ears of corn and add to the pot. Simmer for about 10 minutes, until the corn is soft.

(If you use frozen corn or canned corn, only simmer until heated through—additional cooking time could make the corn tough.)

For a thicker consistency, blend half of the soup and add it back to the pot. Season with salt and pepper. Serve dotted with basil or chive oil or sprinkled with fresh herbs.

Fragrant Herb Oil

HERB-FLAVORED OILS can be used to garnish soups, dip breads, and dress salads.

Ingredients

½ cup packed fresh herbs such as basil, chives, cilantro, or parsley.

1 cup olive oil

Directions

Puree the herbs and oil in a blender until smooth. In a small pot, simmer the mixture over medium heat for one minute. Carefully pour the oil through a fine strainer into a heat-proof container or jar, then strain it again through a coffee filter. Stir the oil as it filters if the filter becomes clogged.

Use oils made with fresh herbs within 24 hours of making. Dilute with more olive oil to desired strength before serving.

Grilled Vegetables

WHETHER YOU COOK THEM indoors or out, these vegetables can be added to soups and make an excellent side dish on their own.

Ingredients
Vegetables of your choice, such as:

Mushrooms
Cherry tomatoes
Bell peppers, cut into pieces
Zucchini, sliced into rounds
Yellow squash, sliced into rounds

Marinade of your choice, such as:

¼ cup olive oil
1 Tb minced garlic
2 Tb lemon juice or red wine vinegar
½ tsp dried oregano
Salt and pepper to taste

Directions

Whisk together marinade ingredients and season with salt and pepper.

If you're grilling, push vegetable pieces onto skewers, then brush each skewer with marinade and place on a baking sheet. If you're using the oven, toss vegetables with marinade in a bowl, then spread coated vegetables onto a baking sheet.

Light your grill or preheat your oven to 400 degrees F while the veggies sit for 15 minutes so the flavor of the marinade can infuse them.

Grill or roast vegetables until tender, approximately 10-12 minutes. Serve warm.

Crime Chowder

BETHANY'S INFAMOUS re-constructed, deconstructed chowder! It's a crowd-pleaser—just leave your pocket pistol out of it.

Ingredients

1 recipe corn chowder

1 recipe grilled vegetables, chopped after cooking

2 cups chopped, cooked cherrystone clams (or two 10-ounce cans baby clams, drained)

1 recipe basil oil

Directions

In a large pot, combine the corn chowder, grilled vegetables, and clams. Bring to a simmer over medium heat, stirring occasionally to prevent scorching.

Serve topped with a few drops of basil oil.

Bethany's Best Cookies

THESE COOKIES ARE AS close to an orange creamsicle as you can get in cookie form! Buttery, melt-in-your mouth little cookies that are great with tea or coffee. While Sharky enjoyed a cookie in the story, these are not for dogs!

Ingredients

1 cup butter (softened to room temperature)

¼ cup sugar

1 cup flour

1 tsp vanilla extract

seeds from ½ vanilla bean (or an additional 1 tsp vanilla extract)

1 tsp fresh orange juice

orange zest

Directions

Heat oven to 350 degrees.

Whip butter and sugar until fluffy. Mix in flour, then add vanilla extract, vanilla bean seeds, orange juice, and orange zest.

Mix well, adding flour if necessary until dough is stiff. Roll into a ball, then pat down into a flat circle. Wrap in plastic wrap and refrigerate for 15 minutes (but no more than 30 or it will be too hard to roll out).

After chilling, roll the dough between sheets of parchment paper to a quarter-inch thick. Use a small glass or round cutter to cut into circles.

Transfer cookies to a parchment-covered baking sheet. Bake 15–20 minutes, until the edges are golden brown. Transfer cookies to a rack to cool.

Yield: 18–24 cookies, depending on how large you make them.

Books by the Author

The Death du Jour Series:

Crime Chowder (Book 1)
    Risky Bisqueness (novella, Book 1.5)
Rest in Split Peas (Book 2)
Chili con Carnage (Book 3)
Lentil Death Do Us Part (Book 4)

• • • •

Other Books by Hillary Avis:

KERNEL OF DOUBT (A Neela Durante Mystery)
    The Season for Slaying (short story)

• • • •

Stay in touch!

WWW.HILLARYAVIS.COM
    hillaryavisauthor@gmail.com
For free books, giveaways, sneak peeks, and early announcements, subscribe to Hillary's Author Updates. http://eepurl.com/dobGAD

Made in the USA
Columbia, SC
17 November 2020